Books by Mildred Cram

Old Seaport Towns
Lotus Salad
Stranger Things
The Tide
Scotch Valley
One-Arm Sutton (with General F.A. Sutton)
Madder Music
Kingdom of Innocents
Forever
The Promise
Born In Time

Mildred Cram

SUNSTONE
PRESS

SANTA FE

Sunstone books may be purchased for educational, business, or sales
promotional use. For information please write: Special Markets Department,
Sunstone Press, P.O. Box 2321, Santa Fe, New Mexico 87504-2321.

Library of Congress Cataloging-in-Publication Data:
Cram, Mildred, 1889-
    Sir : a novel / by Mildred Cram.
        p. cm.
    ISBN 0-86534-339-X (pbk.)
    1. Politicians—Fiction. 2. Man-woman relationships—Fiction.
    I.Title.
PS3505.R2184 S57 2003
813'.52—dc22

                                                        2003020057

Published in

SUNSTONE PRESS
POST OFFICE BOX 2321
SANTA FE, NM 87504-2321 / USA
(505) 988-4418 / ORDERS ONLY (800) 243-5644
FAX (505) 988-1025
WWW.SUNSTONEPRESS.COM

1

Edward always knew when Eithne was about to come downstairs. There was first a rustle along the upstairs hall, then a pause and finally the descent. The taffeta slips she wore accounted for the hissing rustle, but she moved like a snake, not stepping from step to step but coiling down, soundlessly.

"Edward!"

He rejected the unpleasant image and forced himself to see her as a handsome woman of forty, his half-sister. The two halves . . . if that was the genetic composition . . . bore no remote resemblance to one another. Brother and sister belonged to the human race, but there the similarities ended.

"I was just going out," he said.

"Where?"

"I thought of taking a walk."

"A walk?"

"I'm quite up to it."

"The doctor said you were not to go anywhere alone. Not for a week at least."

"I'm quite all right."

"Then I'll go with you."

"Please, no."

She made a gesture that meant: "I give up! You're impossible." And turning away, went smoothly, effortlessly, upstairs again.

Edward saw the backs of her legs in seamless beige, her long body patted and steamed and starved into fashionable grace. "Expensive snake," he thought. And the image took over again.

"I'm leaving tomorrow morning," she called down from the landing. "I suppose I've got to get used to your being alone here."

Edward didn't answer. He tried not to leap at the door, but to open it calmly and to step outside as if he were doing the most natural . . . the *safest* . . . thing in the world.

The wide verandah was in full sunlight. It was warm for an afternoon in March, windless, and not a cloud in the sky. During the summer the lawn would be a lush green, the clover machine-mowed and fragrant, but now it was brown, save where patches of crusty snow melted morosely in the hollows.

Edward followed a bricked path through the rose garden. The bushes wore their winter overcoats; straw and burlap cones were wrapped around the barren stalks. The tool-house was boarded up; it was still too early to spade the frozen earth. No birds. Not a living thing in sight, anywhere.

Edward walked slowly, conscious of a certain lack of balance, a sense of physical confusion, as if nothing worked as it should. The veins in his hands felt full. His heart

2

betrayed him unless he took great care to head off its sudden bursts of speed. He had been ill, exiled to a room in a hospital for six weeks, submitting to the faintly contemptuous attention of doctors who seemed convinced that whatever it was that ailed him their science had no way to get at it. None of these highly paid fellows dared to tell him what they really thought: that his sickness was psychosomatic. Had he been a penniless nobody sweating it out in a ward, they would have made short shrift of his symptoms. Did he hurt here, or there? No. Well, then! We'll test this and that: examine this and that: the brain, the spine, the spleen, the liver. We'll push and prod and photograph and guess . . . Edward could afford it; he was a rich man.

The Press was determined to get at the truth of his condition, and newsmen surged through the hospital, clogging the corridors, monopolizing the phone booths. Could they see him? They could not. Was it true that he was paralyzed? No comment. Was he dying? No comment. Could Mr. Reasoner speak to him for a moment? No one could speak to him.

Finally the pressure was relieved. An official statement was released: the illustrious patient was suffering from a minor concussion, that was all. No injuries: no fractures or burns. A period of complete rest was indicated. Nothing more.

The path frayed out once it had fulfilled its purpose; the neatly spaced bricks gave way to gravel, then wandered into the pine woods that bordered the estate. Here, centuries of fallen needles had made a tawny carpet so thick that neither man nor beast could dent its surface.

Edward hesitated and looked back at the house. From where he stood, the windows were like brass shields flashing in the sun; a thread of smoke rose from one of the tall chimneys. Edward had been born here, in a second-story bedroom, on just such a day as this; he could remember his mother's telling him so: "A warm day . . . there was spring in the air. When you were safely born, I asked to look at you. Oh, Edward, what an ugly baby you were! Who would have believed that you would grow up to be the handsome creature you are!"

He was not handsome, but he had been called "the young Lincoln" too often not to believe that there was some truth in the comparison: the height, the square shoulders, the blackness of hair and the aggressive nose. With the mouth any resemblance ended, and the attraction for women began. Of this, however, Edward was unaware. If he thought of his appearance at all it was with a sort of futile annoyance at being recognized wherever he went. Even those who had no idea who he was stared at him, but those who did recognize him swung in their tracks to have another look. It was like seeing a character step out from the T.V. screen . . . a strange duality . . . Lincoln wearing Welby's tunic or Marshal Dillon's hat.

For this reason, to escape the probing public eye, he had hoped he could hide from the consuming attention of the crowd and in decent privacy arrive at his own conclusions. He had left Washington at night, and abjuring the black limousine that was the symbol of his office, had driven a small, inconspicuous car to New York and had gone immediately to Eithne's house. No one saw him leave and no one saw him arrive; it was a novel experience to stand on Eithne's doorstep at three o'clock in the morning, pressing the doorbell until a cautious man-servant demanded from inside: "Who's there? What do you want?"

Eithne, clutching a wool robe, her eyes blurred with sleep, came from her bedroom to confront him. She was a woman who knew well how to confront.

4

"Where on earth did *you* come from? I thought you were in the hospital."

"I was," he said. And with a faint smile he added: "I'm not. As you see."

"Is anything wrong? Are you worse?"

"I'm quite well."

"Don't be silly. Must you pretend with me?" She made a quick gesture toward a telephone. "I'll call Dr. Brandt."

"You won't. Now, or ever. I'm through with Brandt and he with me. We have washed our hands of each other's failures. I'm on my way to Easterly."

"At this time of year?"

"The first robin . . . a little ahead of schedule! I want you to come with me. You can help me open the house. And then I'll let you go."

"How sweet of you!"

She stared at him with critical eyes, searching for some sign of defection, of mental wavering. He returned the stare, his own eyes steady and kind . . . he could always feel sorry for anyone who tried to trip him; if they succeeded, he could retaliate, and this was perhaps the secret of his strength. He knew what Eithne was thinking and with one of his gentle smiles led her on to saying it: "I should think this was the worst possible time to go off by yourself. You need distraction. People." She broke off and went in search of a cigarette. "Is it too soon to speak to you of having fun? In a quiet way, of course? No one expects you to mourn forever. Or to blame yourself. It wasn't your fault."

"But it was," Edward said.

He looked back once more at the house. Perhaps because Easterly belonged neither to the past nor to the present there was something strangely reassuring about the place. Built by Edward's grandfather in the nineties, it had escaped the swollen bay windows and baroque ornamentation of its period. The green and white awnings were already in place, and it had the look of a Newport "cottage." It stood on the crest of a hill, high enough to afford a view of the lake, yet protected by the circling stand of pines. The greenhouses and stables were at the bottom of the farther slope; once there had been orchids and horses to be cared for, and stablemen and gardeners to care for them. Nowadays, the stalls were empty and the damp sweetness of the greenhouses no longer misted the glass roofs. For many years a gigantic Rolls, black as sin, had stood on jacks in the garage. Edward could not bear to part with it. Once he tried it out on the country roads, but for all its watch-like perfection, it seemed too heavy and he felt vaguely absurd, sitting in high, solitary splendor behind the unfamiliar wheel. Twice a year this mastodon was oiled and waxed, its fierce headlights polished, its upholstery whisked. But Edward drove the caretaker's pick-up truck if he drove at all. Whenever he came to Easterly, he made a quick tour of the estate and was off again.

This time he returned with a definite purpose: like the old Rolls in the garage he meant to jack himself up and wait for a healing. If he could straighten out the confusions in his mind and get his future into focus again . . .

Suddenly, doubt blew across his spirit like a windswept fog. A sense of unreality was coming at him again, blurring and erasing. He took a few steps back toward the house, his heart beating much too fast, his breathing shallow. The retreat was cowardly and he knew it. Eithne would know it, too. He must keep up the pretense of good mental health as he had in the hospital . . . none of the medics had spotted the real reason for his weakness, his sweats, his dry-eyed weeping. Damn! What *ailed* him, that he couldn't face walking alone through a shadowy grove? He had never feared anything . . .

6

except perhaps the sting of a yellow-jacket! War hadn't scared him. But by God he was scared now! Only Eithne mustn't guess. No one must guess. Whatever it was, he must fight it alone. And win. Or lose . . . Well. First things first. He'd go through the wood and down to the lake, even if his knees buckled and he had to crawl. He'd go.

Beneath the pines, the silence was absolute. Only once, faraway somewhere, a crow cawed. Edward thought that men must have heard that sound since the beginning of time. Great civilizations built up and lasted a while and were spent, but the crows went on forever. He wondered whether the bulldozer would destroy them, too, and whether the day would come, and soon, when the crows would be heard no more except in the memories of a few old men?

Once during the war when he was on leave in England, Edward wrote his friend Ricardo and mentioned that he had spent a week in Cornwall and hadn't seen or heard a crow. Plenty of small birds in the hedgerows, but no crows? Why?

Ricardo replied after a month or so . . . correspondence had no continuity in those days . . . and advised Edward to look up an old phonograph record that would very likely help him over his crow-less years! "An aspirin for nostalgia," he wrote. "Somehow it captures the feeling of an English garden just before dawn . . . mist, moonlight, nightingales, the distant barking of a farm dog, and then with dawn the crow sound. Find it, Edward, and play it when you're lonely for Easterly and youth. If this doesn't work, I'll ask Robert Frost to write a poem . . . I wonder, has he ever celebrated the immortal crow? He should. He will, if it's for you. You know, he thinks a lot of you. He thinks you may have something big to do for America . . ."

Edward's property was wire-fenced all the way around except for the lake frontage. The main highway turned inland beyond the village, and from there only an unpaved road, rough and weed-grown, skirted the lake. A sign, *"Private Property"* may have prevented a few timid souls from trespassing, but in summer, campers and picnic-parties made use of the beach. The entrance to Easterly itself was kept barred by an iron gate between tall fieldstone posts. A caller could give his name and state his business over the telephone from the village; if he was welcome, someone would come down from the house and admit him with a fine clanking of chains and bars. There was no other way to keep the place clear of those who consider the home of any public character their own to enjoy and deface. Edward never knew how these people found him out, but they did. And they would again if the press discovered his whereabouts; the reprieve from a pitiless publicity might not last much longer.

Here in the shadowy silence of the wood, he was more than ever aware of how tense he was, every nerve and muscle braced against thinking of the accident. He made a deliberate effort to relax, stretching his spine and thrusting his chin out, then letting go, only to build up the painful rigidity again. The medics had prescribed sedatives but these Edward had refused. He had always fought against surrendering any part of consciousness; for this reason, perhaps, he was never flagged down by liquor and disliked sleep if it carried him too far away from awareness; four hours were enough to recharge a battery that was never wholly spent no matter how hard he worked. He had learned this by observing certain men under fire, one in particular who could black out in the midst of chaos, bolt upright, eyes open, but for a split-second sound asleep. And so, restored.

Edward did this now, or tried to do it; leaning against a tree, pressing his back against the rough, cold bark, he gazed up into the motionless boughs and summoned forgetfulness. But he couldn't escape the threat that stalked him; the terrifying threat of a compulsive move upon self-destruction.

8

Eithne was not a woman given to hen-clucking domestic anxieties, but when the sun disappeared behind the pines she began a restless tour of the rooms; Edward had gone out for this "walk" of his two hours ago. He should be back by now. And yet she hesitated to alarm the caretaker and his wife. A glance at the clock on the mantel in the hall did nothing to reassure her; it said *seven*. Then she realized that it hadn't been wound; the pendulum was motionless and the gilt figures supporting the face seemed exhausted by the futility of their service. With lifted arms they upheld years of lost time.

Eithne slipped her fingers under the clock and found the key. After a few turns a gritty ticking announced a return to life and the clock struck seven . . . never before with such a furious, ear-shattering clang.

"Damn it, you frightened me," Eithne said. "Who do you think you are? Big Ben?"

She hoped that Mrs. Littlefield hadn't heard her swear . . . she never did unless she lost her temper.

The caretaker's wife came in from the kitchen. "What on earth was *that*?"

Eithne pointed to the clock, too shaken to answer.

"It's ten to five," Mrs. Littlefield said. With the tip of an arthritic finger she turned back the hands. "He said supper at five. I'm fixing apple turnovers for him. They don't wait, once they've risen. Isn't he coming?"

Eithne went to the window, and Mrs. Littlefield followed her. The two women stood side by side looking out across the cold dry brownness of the lawn into the last rays of the sun. There was no sign of Edward and Eithne recalled what Dr. Brandt had said about the possibility of suicide. "Watch for any signs of a total withdrawal from reality. He has had a severe shock and will try to escape from something that shouldn't have happened, but did happen. There's a sort of

9

psychic wound; healing may be slow, but it needn't leave a scar. It won't, unless he finds the suffering unendurable. In that case he might take his own way out."

"I don't think he looks very well," Mrs. Littlefield said. "Mr. Littlefield and I both remarked on it. Of course he's grieving. But we can't grieve forever. It's not natural."

"No," Eithne said.

"When the young President was shot, the whole world grieved. But after awhile people put it out of mind . . . not that they forgot. They just pushed it down and covered it up. It was over. It was *history*."

"Yes," Eithne said again.

Mrs. Littlefield went back toward the kitchen, but Eithne stopped her.

"You'll stay here and take care of him, won't you?"

"I suppose so," Mrs. Littlefield said after a pause. "But I thought he'd send for his own help. Mr. Littlefield and I don't care for being in service. We're not young enough any more . . ."

"Just for a few days! You'll stay here in the house, of course? He shouldn't be alone at night."

"We couldn't do that. We have our own house in the village, and a cat and nursing kittens we can't leave. We'll come first thing in the morning and do what we can for him. But no, once the sun's down, we go home. I'm sorry, but that's that. Fond as we are of him and grateful for all he's done for us."

Eithne said nothing; she recognized the New Englander's stubborn resistance to discipline . . . it would be useless to insist. As for Edward's sending for the half-dozen servants who had followed him from post to post for years, it wasn't likely that they'd stay long in the Victorian country-house. Well, coming here was Edward's own idea. Eithne had no

10

intention of giving up her own pursuits to make her brother's stupid flight from heartache comfortable.

Restless again, really apprehensive now, she rustled from room to room, lighting lamps against the deepening twilight. She had never liked Easterly, except in mid-summer when the cottages and hotels along the lake-shore were occupied and the roads hummed with traffic. And of course, when Edward was governor the old mansion had served as a summer Statehouse and the constant coming and going of people, the colorful garden, the sweep of fragrant lawn, the receptions and dinners erased the sense of remoteness — and for a few months Easterly was at the center of important happenings.

But then Edward began his service in Europe. As ambassador he was useful, but he disliked the devious devices and subterfuges of diplomacy and was never quite adjusted to life in the formal embassies; he was too American, physically and mentally, to blend with the decor. Eithne responded to his call for help and flew over to act as hostess for her bachelor brother. She was determined to rescue him from ambitious women who saw themselves lifted to the heights he was certain to scale. Eithne knew how to detach their predatory fingers. She made enemies, but she also made herself indispensable to Edward. Until he married Valerie.

Eithne paused in the library, a room that reflected the tastes and pursuits of her father and grandfather. The portrait of a great-grandfather wearing the uniform of an officer of the Revolution hung above the white marble mantel, but most of the wall-space was given over to cabinets and bookshelves. The cabinets contained trophies and a display of rifles and hunting knives; the books, well bound, mellow, were beautiful in themselves. Like the worn velvet arm chairs and sofas, the room was vaguely shabby in spite of an air of

11

luxury, something modern designers can't achieve for all their access to old furniture and fabrics. The ornaments . . . oversized crackled jars and bronze candlesticks with flat crystal pendants . . . were probably valuable. Eithne wondered what would happen to them in case Easterly were ever sold . . . There would be no place for them either in the Georgetown house, which Edward owned, or in the modern setting she had contrived for herself in New York. Everything belonging to Easterly . . . even the paintings . . . would probably be put up at auction. The small Burne-Jones, the Watts, the more recent Childe Hassam, the portrait of Edward's mother, painted by Shinn in the Forties, just before she died . . . Easterly would die, too, if Edward did.

Once more the word "suicide" attacked Eithne's consciousness like a vicious-toothed bat. It was all she could do not to strike out with both hands in panic-stricken revulsion. Edward a suicide? Surely, that fine, sound mind of his hadn't been weakened by the tragedy . . . he was still grief-stricken, of course, and that was what she had felt − not a breaking down of his will to live. He had seemed calm enough during the long drive from New York, had handled the car with his usual skill, driving too fast as he always did, but with hands firm on the wheel, and eyes steady. Sitting beside him, wrapped in her furs, Eithne had relaxed, had even dozed. Was this a man who would sacrifice a lifetime of effort and accomplishment? Yet there had been something . . . something deep in him, out of reach, a *difference* . . . Why in God's name had she let him come here? Why hadn't she sent for Ricardo . . . some friend strong enough to help? She couldn't do it, herself; she hadn't the pity or the knowledge or the selfless love. And she thought that perhaps it would have been better had the war snuffed him out years ago. Better than a cowardly death now, with all the ugliness to follow: inquests, headlines, questionings, a hurried, shame-faced funeral, a flag for a hero but no wreath, no laurel, for an immortal.

Besides, what would happen to her, to Eithne? She had planned to step back into his need of her now that Valerie and the boys were gone. He would never again live in the Georgetown house, but she would; she could be a great help to him there, entertaining the right people, the "important" people. A nod from Eithne meant that you were "in," and while she wasn't particularly political-minded, she knew everything there was to know about protocol. She had considerable power of her own, but it would mean nothing if she were to lose Edward. Particularly now that he was only a few short steps from the summit. She had always sensed this, but losing him had seemed an unlikely disaster, until today.

Edward stayed in the grove for a long time. Once, noticing a small white object thrusting through the matted carpet of pine needles, he knelt and uncovered an Indian Pipe, freed it, and for a long time contemplated the miracle of its growth. The stem, blanched from a winter beneath the snow, curved like a swan's neck. Edward realized the plant's beauty but there was no response in his heart; his recognition of it began in the intellect and ended there. This was frightening enough . . . to remember an emotion but to be unable to feel it . . . and Edward, getting to his feet, hurried away from the spot as if the Indian Pipe were a poisonous viper. He was not yet at the bottom of despair, but he was close to it. So far . . . and he was certain of this . . . he hadn't behaved like a madman, hadn't worn his coat backwards or switched his shoes from right to left or slipped into babbling incoherencies. Some inner voice kept right on dictating what gestures he should make, what words he should speak to appear normal. Only the horrible thing about it was that he heard himself speaking and saw himself behaving as if he were on

13

the *outside* of himself . . . a solipsist in reverse? Sitting in judgment upon himself he took great care to censor any indication of self-pity, or to admit, ever, that a rug had been pulled out from under him and that he had fallen flat on his face at the foot of the throne. A stranger had said to him once: "You've had it too easy. All the breaks. If you ever come up against it . . . really up against it . . . boy, it'll go hard with you!" At the time, he had put the outburst down to that curious resentment aroused in certain men by handsewn shoes and well-cut jackets . . . as if filthy overalls were a guarantee of noble purposes and a stained necktie meant you were a good fellow. He wondered, now, if perhaps his critic had been right: at his birth all the ingredients of well-being had been shaken out of the cornucopia: inherited wealth, physical stamina, solid forbears, an ingrained, deep-rooted belief in the essential rightness of his country. Well. None of these gifts made him sacrosanct. He had been spit upon by mobs, splattered with eggs, hissed at. Woven into the popular applause, like steel wire in a braid of hemp, there had been hatred enough to cut his hands to the bone as he climbed. But climb he had. And might again. If only he could find a reason to!

He had come to the edge of the wood and could now see the lake, calm save close in shore where little waves broke with monotonous regularity against the beach. Across the silvery water, a chain of hills, heavily wooded, were nowadays a sanctuary for small game . . . too many gun-happy hunters had all but exterminated the wildlife there. Edward had hunted as a youngster, accepting it as a sport because his father and grandfather did. But he was responsible for the bill that ruled slaughter out of the district for fifty years to come. There were deer there now . . . the beavers were at work again, the skunks and squirrels and porcupines had ventured back . . . there were even a few red foxes and small bear . . .

Edward slid down a bank, crossed the beach and went out to the end of the Easterly dock. He stood there for a long time, unaware that the sun was almost gone, and that a chill current of air had begun to drift along the shore, trailing with it shreds of night mist. He heard the chuckle of water around the piles beneath him but didn't look down. It was deep this far out and would be cold. He began involuntarily to imagine drowning . . . the plunge, the struggle, the final letting go.

Then he saw that someone had come along the beach and was trying to attract his attention. It was a girl wearing slacks and a bulky red sweater. She was dripping wet, as if she had just stepped out of the lake. Even from where he stood he could hear the slush of water in her rubber-soled sneakers.

She called up to him: "Will you help me? A man's hurt, His car turned over. He's trapped. He'll drown if we don't get him out!"

"Drown?"

"The car rolled into the lake. Please come. Please *hurry*!"

Edward ran back along the dock and jumped off into the sand beside her. She ran ahead and there was nothing to do but to follow her. Apparently she hadn't recognized him and for this he was grateful; he hated being pinned like a specimen to some stranger's collection of celebrities. This girl was intent not on him but on the car which had righted itself and now stood half-submerged about fifty feet off shore. The driver was under the wheel, his left arm across the door, a bloody hand trailing in the water.

The nausea of shock was at the pit of Edward's stomach again, and he hesitated at the water's edge, debating whether to go to the injured man's rescue or to turn and run for help.

"I tried," the girl said. "I *couldn't*! But I *tried* . . ."

So. There was no help for it. Edward peeled off his coat, removed his shoes. The first step into the icy water made him recoil and stooping to conceal his reaction he tugged at his socks. Then, barefoot, he waded out, the girl splashing, half-swimming beside him.

"Go back!" he shouted.

She shook her head and kept right on.

The man in the car was only half-conscious, but he attempted a jaunty grin when he saw Edward.

"Fancy meeting *you* here!" he said. Then, with a wash of pallor, he fainted.

As Edward struggled to release and lift the heavy body, he thought that if anyone were trapped it was he, himself. He got the man back to the beach and put him down where a bank of sand offered some protection and support. The girl followed. Her teeth were chattering, her lips blue beneath the smeared-on crimson of her lipstick. She brought Edward's coat and he covered the unconscious fellow as well as he could. Then she went back for the shoes and socks and handed them to Edward.

"What were you doing on this road?" he demanded. "Didn't you see the sign back there?"

"Yes. We saw it."

"Then why didn't you turn around? What were you after?"

"A story," she said. "You, of course! We're reporters."

"I see," he said. "very well. There's a doctor in the village. I'll call him from the house. It won't take long. Wait here."

He turned abruptly and hurried back toward Easterly along an old shortcut he knew that by-passed the pines. Almost obliterated by a tangle of frozen weeds and thorny bushes, the path was steep and rough. Edward crashed through, taking long strides. It was almost dark now and the lake mist was drifting up, clinging, breaking loose again, leaving torn shreds as if a company of tattered ghosts had

16

passed. A castanet-rattling of frogs in a damp hollow ceased abruptly, then began again. Of course those two on the beach were scout ants staking out a lump of sugar for their colony! No use to ask them for a few days' grace; the rest of the horde would arrive tomorrow and the public flaying would begin again: that pitiless exposure which was like being skinned alive . . . a laying bare of lungs, heart, viscera, veins, nerves. And he recalled a statue he had seen somewhere of a martyred saint neatly and expertly deprived of his flesh which he held like a toga, and with a certain elegance, over his arm.

Edward had reached the top of the slope when he heard the girl behind him. He didn't look back or speak, since he had expected this to happen: she would try to get into the house. Let the man on the beach bleed to death; this was a scoop . . . she'd get in, or else! Edward heard again the sloshing sneakers, her quick panting breath. "My dog's in this thicket somewhere," she gasped. "He was frightened. He swam ashore and ran off . . . His name's Murphy."

Edward made a contemptuous sound, a sort of snort of disbelief. He heard her calling: "Murphy! Murphy!" And hoped that she had turned back. Cutting across the rose garden to the brick walk, he saw Easterly glowing with lights. As he hurried up the steps and across the verandah to the door, the girl caught up with him again.

Eithne was warming herself at the fire in the hallway. She held a cup of coffee which she stirred slowly, the gesture expressing annoyance, indignation and resolve. She was wearing her furs. A pillbox the size of a cake of Pear's Soap was poised behind the silver upsurge of her pompadour.

"I'm driving back to New York tonight," she said before Edward could explain. "I can't take the responsibility . . ."

She broke off, suddenly aware of her brother's extra-

17

ordinary appearance and of the girl who had come in with him.

"Edward! Where on *earth* . . .?"

Edward veered away from the word "accident." He used a strangely dated substitute: "There's been a . . . mishap. A car overturned on the lake road. A man's hurt. Badly, I'm afraid."

He made an awkward gesture, glancing quickly at the shivering girl.

"My sister, Mrs. Wade."

The girl would have offered her hand but the coffee cup presented an obstacle. She smiled at Eithne instead. She had very white teeth and Edward was aware of a flash of mischief and good humor.

"My name's Megan," she said. "Megan Donahue. I wonder could I stand in front of the fire? I'm frozen."

Eithne moved quickly.

"Of course. *Edward* . . .?"

It was a cry for help, but Edward had no intention of coming to his sister's rescue. He snatched up the telephone and while he struggled with the mysteries of area codes and information the two women watched him, Eithne with amazement as if he had changed character, the girl with shining eyes as if she were looking at an archangel.

It was after midnight when he finally went to bed. Eithne had gone taking the girl with her, the village doctor had transferred the wounded man to the nearest hospital and now Easterly was silent, the long wings dark. The lake mist had thickened; a muffling fog shrouded the house, dripped from the branches of trees, drenched the walks. Edward was alone.

This was what he had wanted, wasn't it? Well, wasn't it the whole purpose of his flight from Washington? To be alone? In the hospital, there was always a coming and going of

18

doctors and nurses, someone to watch him, quick to spring at him with the everlasting query: "Are you feeling better, sir?" Better! Hah! Their real concern was with the window six stories above the sidewalk where he had been found leaning on the sill staring down with what might have been a purpose. There had been panic in the corridors, an urgent clamor of voices paging Dr. Brandt over the loud speakers.

"Dr. Brandt, please. *Emergency*!"

"Surely, Edward," the startled physician said, "you weren't thinking of jumping out? You know, you aren't the only man to have lost his wife and children tragically. Better face up to it at once, before it sinks its fangs into your mind." And Edward had said: "I'll deal with it in my own way, in my own good time. Right now, I want very much to go home to Easterly."

And here he was.

Halfway upstairs he noticed that he had left the library lamp lighted. He went back and turned it off, remembering that when he was a child he had been afraid of the dark. His father was contemptuous of such cowardice and ignored it, but his mother used to tiptoe down as soon as her husband was asleep and switch on the library lamp. A faint wedge of light would appear on the ceiling of Edward's room at the top of the stairs and the terrified boy would come out from under the bedclothes.

When he was seven his father said to him: "I know your mother gives in to you. Perhaps she doesn't care if you grow up to be a coward. But I do. You can't expect me to be your friend until you've conquered this fear of the dark. When you have, tell me. I'll believe you. One thing I'm sure of: you're honest." And that night, as soon as his mother had performed her merciful deed, Edward slipped down and turned off the lamp.

This was the way it had been ever since; whenever he feared anything he forced himself to grope for courage in the total dark. Courage. If you could kindle even a pinpoint of *that* light you could swing it ahead of you like an electric flash and so keep to the path. This was why he had left the hospital and the starched guardians of his safety, talking his way out with such disarming logic and cheerful charm that the entire staff agreed that it was the thing to do. A week's rest in the country, then back to his desk! It remained for the Press to accept this. There had been rumors of a mental breakdown. Suspicious members of the Opposition bayed like hunting dogs across the fields of conjecture . . . And already a pair of reporters was at his heels! The rest couldn't be far behind . . .

He climbed the stairs slowly, seeing well enough by the last ruddy flicker of the fire in the hallway. A log broke in two and collapsed in a shower of sparks. Then there was only the rustle of hot ashes on the hearth.

His bedroom had been furnished for the heir to millions, and Edward had always disliked it . . . the heavy mahogany bed with its plump, dark red coverlets, the vast bureau, the velvet curtains . . . all of it stuffy and melancholy. There was a scent of camphor and in the adjoining bathroom a lingering trace of lavender. Mrs. Littlefield had filled the racks with linen hand-towels and over-sized bath-towels. But she hadn't turned back the bedclothes or unpacked Edward's suitcase; these were menial duties once the privilege of a proud dynasty of family servants. Nor had Mr. Littlefield laid a fire; he had dumped an armload of kindling and a few pine logs on the hearth and left it at that.

Edward made ready for bed, ignoring his reflection in the bathroom mirror. This was a habit of his. He disliked being reminded that his face was a sort of Party trademark, like the

20

elephant and the donkey. Someone had said of him that he was larger than life and twice as real . . . a cartoonist's delight. He scrubbed and splashed now as if to rid himself of the lake water that somehow seemed unclean because that fellow had bled into it.

He lay for a long time testing and disciplining his thoughts. The urge to kill himself hadn't recurred since that moment in the wood and his flight to the end of the dock. He had been startled out of his almost-realized intention by the girl's voice, and ever since had been relieved of the agony.

Eithne had decided that he was past the danger of cracking up, and that she could relax. Only first she must see to it that this girl didn't try to spend the night . . . she was obviously the sort who would, at the drop of a hat. And to Edward's surprise, his sister had suddenly switched to cordiality: "I'll drive you back to New York, Miss Donahue. You can wear one of my coats. And Edward will let you have a shirt and a pair of socks. Mrs. Littlefield will show you where you can change. Only don't be too long. It's quite late."

"Thank you," the girl said, and followed the caretaker's wife.

"She can't stay here, of course," Eithne said.

"Why not?"

Eithne shrugged. "She's very pretty."

"Is she?"

"Besides, dear Edward, she'd make capital of the situation. I know her kind. They're a dime a dozen in Washington. Little nymphs with an eye out for important men."

Edward smiled.

"Yes. I mean you! Now more than ever!" Eithne broke off, aware that she had crossed into forbidden territory: Dr. Brandt had warned her not to remind Edward of his loss.

"Don't worry," she said quickly, with an executive smile, "I'll get rid of her."

When the girl reappeared, wearing Eithne's coat, Edward realized that she was indeed very pretty. He had seen girls like her in Ireland, with smudged-in, black-lashed gray eyes and flushed cheeks. Halfway down the stairs she paused to look at a painting . . . a misty river and a blurred moon . . . one of half a dozen small canvases banked on the stair wall. It was the briefest pause but it served to steady her for Eithne's inspection.

"If you're ready, Miss Donahue? Shall we go?"

Eithne kissed Edward's cheek. "Goodbye, dear. Take care of yourself. And let me know if you change your mind about staying here. You will! I give you a week at most!"

The girl hung back long enough to take Edward's outstretched hand. "Goodbye. Look for my dog, won't you? I'll call tomorrow. And if you find him, I'll come back for him. Remember, his name's Murphy."

"Murphy," Edward repeated.

For a moment, clasping hands, they regarded each other. There were things the girl might have said . . . the usual, expected things. She didn't say any of them, yet Edward had the impression that she was sorry for what had happened.

"I hope your friend's going to be all right," he said politely.

"He's not my friend," she said. "I met him in a bar day before yesterday. But Murphy *is* my friend! He's big and silly and brave and full of love . . . Find him, please!"

It was probably a trick. A way of getting back to Easterly. And yet Edward lay awake listening for the barking of a dog. He found himself wondering whether there had been something sinister about the girl and her companion; they certainly weren't reporters of the trench coat variety . . .

22

Whatever their purpose, they had failed so far to hurt anyone but themselves. The village doctor had called back to say that the wounded man would recover but that he had had a close call. Who would be responsible for the expenses? And Edward had said promptly: "I will, of course. The accident happened on my property. They hit a rut as deep as an Alpine crevasse." The doctor snorted and asked what they were doing that far off the highway and at that hour? "Were they after you, Edward? Ever since Kennedy's death I've been concerned about you." It was Edward's turn to snort. "Me? Nonsense. No one wants to kill me." The doctor remarked that this was perhaps so. "Not yet, perhaps. But in a year or so . . . Well, we'll search the car in the morning. We might find evidence. I understand Eithne drove the girl back to New York. I hope she was smart enough to notify the police. This whole thing smells, Edward!"

"Did *you*?" Edward asked.

"Did I what?"

"Notify the police?"

"No. I confess I didn't."

"Then don't. I came up here to get some peace."

"Peace," the doctor said, "isn't likely. Not for you. A man who deliberately chooses to live the life of a public servant is grist for the mob's mill. You should have known this when you entered politics."

The doctor's voice suggested that he was smiling a reluctant Down-East smile.

"I've known you since the day you were born, Edward. I slapped your bottom and swung you by your heels and started you on your way. At times I wish I hadn't. At other times I'm glad I did. Once in a while you show signs of being the sort of timber we need."

"Thanks," Edward said. He was about to add that he no longer cared what timber was used or what was built . . . if anything! The habit of reticence persisted, however, and he said instead: "Let's keep the police out of this, shall we?"

"Very well. If I can . . ."

The doctor broke off. And then, embarrassed by his own profound sympathy, he said awkwardly how sorry he had been to hear of Edward's loss. "Call me if I can be of help. Are you alone out there?"

"Quite alone."

"You were right to come to Easterly. The gale is strong, but here your roots go deep. Let's hope they'll serve to hold you steady."

"Your roots go deep." Edward thought that this might be true, although he had pulled his own roots free of Easterly easily enough when he was ready to explore the rest of the world. He thought now of the innumerable rooms along the wings, all of them kept as clean and polished as they were when the family lived here, and filled with inherited treasures . . . nothing ever to be discarded, sold, given away. To walk from room to room was like visiting a museum stocked with family treasures: relics of the early settlement, the Revolution, the Civil War and on through the Victorian to the hideous splendor of the Nineties. A Tiffany glass chandelier swung above a Chippendale dining-room table and a silver service said to have been designed by Paul Revere shared the sideboard with an array of *L'Art Nouveau* platters and candlesticks. Someone . . . Edward's grandmother, perhaps . . . had had a passion for pincushions and these were still displayed in her bedroom, bristling like velvet and satin porcupines. Some member of the family had lived for a long time in Italy and had brought back a fine Venetian screen, pale silver-gold and green, and a set of Florentine chairs upholstered in worn ruby velvet. Books and paintings were everywhere. Bronzes and altar-lamps. Oriental rugs and brass fire screens and two magnificent Steinways standing back to

24

back in the music room . . .

All of these things reflected a way of life, now as obsolete as the vast pantries where sets of Sevres and Haviland were stored behind glass, and crystal glittered obscurely on shelves that reached to the ceiling. Edward could remember the kitchen when two cooks ruled there . . . absolute sovereigns of their own territory. He could remember dinner-parties given by his grandmother, and served with a ritualistic formality that would seem wasted nowadays . . . so much effort to create a mood as impermanent as smoke! Where were the lace covers and doilies and gigantic embroidered napkins now? Stored away in drawers, turning faintly yellow with lack of use . . . And upstairs there were closets and cupboards filled with linen sheets, blankets, cases, stack upon stack, all neatly folded and tied with satin ribbons, never to know sunlight or fresh air again . . .

Edward had inherited all of these things; they belonged to him and not to Eithne, who had exchanged her interest in the estate for the greater security of a trust. Tax-wise, Easterly had eaten into Edward's fortune, but for some reason . . . sentimental perhaps . . . he hadn't sold it. He wondered, now, whether he ever would, or whether he'd settle down here "in the tradition." The phrase made him smile in the dark. As a tradition, Easterly belonged to a past already remote. It projected a musty image in spite of its order and shine and elegance. A contemporary tradition was in the making. What would Easterly appear to be to those destined to look back at it fifty years from now? It had seemed beautiful to those who built and furnished it, and they themselves had seemed impressive, important, enviable. Would today's cubes of steel and glass come to mean "home" to the next generation? Or would they be bulldozed out of existence before they had had time to take on the patina of this century? Edward had gone along with the modern; he was not a carper given to indiscriminate criticism of anything new. Things happening today had always stimulated him because they were unfamiliar. Why, then, had he returned to Easterly? It must have been his conviction that he could no longer cope with the pressures of his position. Too many problems. Too much responsibility. Too much expected of him. The duties and obligations had accumulated over the years until he was enmeshed in them like that trapped lion of the fables. And where was the mouse to gnaw him free? It could be Easterly, retirement, a deliberate indifference to what elder statesmen speak of as the call to duty. It could be that he must turn away from the things to be dealt with: a decline of standards, a loss of direction . . . the machine . . . war . . . the surge of violence, drink, drugs, sex . . . the mounting human tide . . . restlessness, rebellion and racial hatreds . . . He turned on his side and pounded the pillows making a hollow for his head. But he could find no comfortable spot; it was coming again, the memory he must erase from consciousness . . . it began as a physical tension in his arms, then caught at the back of his neck. He felt a throbbing weight behind his eyes. He sat up kicking off the coverlets and, clasping his knees with both arms, put his head down on them. He mustn't remember! *He mustn't remember!*

But then he seemed to be standing beside the plane on the airfield at Charleston, and, once surrendered to the vision, had to go on with it.

He had flown down from Washington in his twin-engined Cessna to pick up Valerie and the boys. They had been spending a fortnight with Valerie's grandmother in her house on Legare Street, and were being driven out to the field to meet him. He saw the car, coming very fast, and with the usual leap of his heart waved a greeting. Valerie got out and ran toward him, the boys at her side. She was dressed in white, her shining hair loose. She motioned to the driver to wait, and when Edward leaned down to kiss her, pushed him away with a strong thrust of both hands.

"We mustn't fly," she said, her breath coming in short gasps. "Haven't you heard? Everyone's been warned to stay indoors . . ."

"I know," Edward said quietly.

"Listen to me!" she cried. "This is a hurricane! Or didn't you know?"

"I'll fly ahead of it," Edward interrupted. "Get in. All three of you! And hurry."

Valerie shook her head. She gave Edward a strange look, almost as if she hated him. He had seen that look only once before, when he lifted her veil at the altar the day of their marriage. Something in her eyes that seemed to say: "You won't control me, now or ever. I belong to myself and always will."

"I'll go with you," she said. "The boys, no! They stay here with their grandmother."

"Where's your luggage?"

"I left it at the house."

She turned and gathered the boys close, her arms around them. The sky had darkened. Small spirals of wind put down, twisted, raced across the field. Two men tumbled out of a transport plane and ran toward the hangar. No one else was in sight.

"Please trust me, Valerie," Edward said. "It's a lot safer to fly. Your grandmother's house is more likely to fall apart than this plane." He put his hand on the Cessna's flank, as a rider might touch his mount; he felt the powerful vibrations of the metal along his arm and knew the confidence of a flier who had never cracked up . . . not in fifty wartime missions, nor since.

He turned abruptly and signaled to the driver of the waiting car: "Go on back!" The car turned, the tires

27

squeaking. It sped away toward the city.

Valerie let her arms fall from her sons' shoulders. She watched them scramble into the plane, as perhaps the mothers of the Innocents surrendered their young to the slicing swords of the assassins. Edward slapped their hard little behinds to boost them up. They were tall boys for their age . . . only six and eight . . . and sturdy. They settled into their places, their eyes bright, their cheeks flushed. But when Edward turned to offer Valerie his hand, he saw that she was very pale, and the hand she gave him was cold. The sky had darkened suddenly and drops of rain began to fall like lead pellets; there was a smell of dust and sulphur in the air, and a distant thrumming sound seemed to roll around the horizon and to encircle the field. At that moment Edward might have turned back. A sort of jerk ran through his body as if a string had been pulled by an unseen hand. He started to speak, to say that he was sorry . . . if she was frightened, of course they'd try to get back to the city . . . But then he realized that this was something between Valerie and himself; it had nothing to do with the onrushing hurricane or with the danger ahead: she must believe in him and trust him and go with him, unquestioning, as women who love go with the men they love.

"Please trust me, Valerie."

"Very well. I will."

That was all. She took her place beside him. Now they were together, mother, father, sons. The take-off was smooth except for a shudder as a gust of wind struck like a slap against the Cessna's side. Then they were clear and lifting easily. As always Edward responded to the plane's obedience to his will. He had discovered that he could love a mechanical thing if he could animate and control it. A feeling of exultation overcame any doubt he may have had.

28

"Don't worry," he said, turning his head briefly to glance at Valerie, "we'll make it. And then you'll be glad. Charleston's going to take a beating, but Washington's in the clear."

The boys were staring out through the suddenly drenched and streaming window into a blackness that was blacker than night . . . and only a moment ago the sun had been shining in a blur of vapour! The plane wavered, lurched, dropped, climbed again, shuddering, fighting for altitude.

"So soon," Edward heard himself say. "Where did it come from? How did this happen?"

He knew when she reached over and put her hand out to the boys. He knew when she told them it was going to be all right . . . their father would get them safely home.

Then they were driving through a wall of ice, encased in a sound like the splintering and crackling of broken glass, and out again into a fraction of calm when the plane steadied and balanced. At that moment Edward realized that he had no control whatever; the hurricane had taken over and was playing with this floating object as if it were a leaf whirled and tossed and driven along a gutter. A jagged flash of lightning cut through the dark: tangles and loops of fire, worm-like, writhed on the wings. The Cessna tilted again, slid sideways into a void, dropping endlessly down and down and down . . .

Did Valerie scream? Did he, himself, cry out? Probably not. It was too quick, that last plunge, that plummet drop into chaos and silence.

And then there was the groping toward consciousness. The shattered plane lay like a shot bird in a deep gully, one wing crumpled, the other lifted against a sky the color of mustard. The shrieking wind, full of branches, fence posts, shingles, tin roofs, bricks, spared the gulley its violent blast but not the horrible sound of its passage.

29

Edward shouted: "Valerie! David! Gardner! And on his hands and knees crawled toward them. Valerie lay on her back, sprawled as if disjointed. The boys lay beside her, white, bloodless as split fish . . .

Edward remembered, now, kneeling beside them, and then flinging himself on top of them as if the warmth of his body could bring them back to life. And how he had loved them and pitied them. And had wept and kissed their cold flesh . . .

And then the diminishing howl of the storm, like all hell sucked down a drain pipe. And silence broken by the dry clacking of a searching helicopter's blades. And the pain gathering behind his eyes. *"It was my fault."*

He sprang out of bed, put on his trousers and ran down to the library. Fumbling for the switch he found that there was none; he had to light the lamp on the table. By its shaded glow he opened one of the cases and chose a revolver that had belonged to his father. It felt heavy and cold against his palm. He thought . . . without really thinking . . . that the case should be locked up in case the boys should spend the summer here . . . But the boys weren't coming and never would come! All the plans for their future had been canceled. Loading the revolver he felt momentarily released from suffering, as if with the resolve to use this means he had at last found an escape from self. For a moment he was immersed in radiant relief, absolved. "Now I can forget all of it. I needn't think of how it happened, or why, or my own part in it. I don't respect life any more, so why question the right or wrong of doing away with my own?" And he thought calmly that he'd go back to the grove and do it there, where it was still and dark . . . It would be good to let his blood sink into the soil that nourished the trees . . . his soil, and theirs.

He left the lamp lighted, and slipping the revolver into his

30

pocket, went across the hallway to the verandah door. As he opened it, he saw that the fog had turned into a soft, steady, cold rain. Across the wet porch, at the top of the steps, wagging apologetically, stood a large, black dog.

Man and dog stared at each other for a moment. Then Edward said: "Come here, fellow." But the dog didn't respond; the tail stopped wagging and the moist black nose rotated as if on the scent of possible betrayal.

"Murphy," Edward said, trying out the name, and the dog came to him, pushed against his outstretched hand. He was a heavy young brute, strong as a bull, and Edward almost lost balance.

"You'd better come inside," he said. The dog was wearing a collar and there was a clinking of metal tags. Edward hooked his fingers under the tight leather and began to pull the big fellow toward the door. He needn't have bothered. Murphy wanted in. So Edward followed his guest to the kitchen and fed him warm milk and crumbled bread. The dog splashed the food on Mrs. Littlefield's immaculate floor. As Edward waited and watched, he was rewarded by warm upward glances and dog smirks and a slow, yet appreciative motion of the heavy tail . . . a sort of promissory note: *I'll really wag for you when this is over. Don't expect too much in the meantime.* Then he began to shiver and Edward fetched some tea cloths and dropped them over the wet body and rubbed until Murphy lifted a hind leg and scratched his belly in ecstacy . . . In the meantime, the revolver in Edward's pocket sagged, heavy with portent, dragging down the stuff of his jacket into an ugly bulge. "I guess we'll put this thing back," he said aloud. "Come, Murphy. We're going to bed."

The black dog followed him into the library and then upstairs. Holding his great, hard dog-head to one side, he watched Edward undress, trying to understand, to make certain of welcome. When the man crawled back under the tossed-off covers, the dog came close and put his muzzle within reach of a possible stroking. Edward obliged. Murphy quivered all over; his eyes brimmed with the most ingratiating love and trust. He wanted up.

"All right," Edward said at last. "Come along."

He lay back on the pillows, and gave his face to Murphy's rapturous tongue. It was little enough to do, after all, in gratitude for a stay of execution.

2

When Edward woke it was past dawn. Rain had poured in through the open windows during the night and the curtains were soggy wet. The dog was gone.

Then Edward heard what had awakened him. Voices down stairs. Loud laughter and a rattle of dishes coming from the direction of the kitchen. Someone must have left the pantry door open, because there was a smell of bacon and coffee even up here. Pleasant enough sounds and smells. But who at this hour of the morning had broken through the locked gate? Edward thought that the pack was truly baying at his heels, but that it would be useless to cower like a cornered quarry. Better see for himself what was going on . . .

Not waiting to shave, he hurried down. Someone had built a fire in the hallway and a man was standing with his back turned to the blaze . . . a youngish gray-blond fellow with what turned out to be a perpetual smile, an upturn at the corners of his mouth. He glanced at Edward, but didn't move.

"Good morning, sir," he said. Edward hadn't recognized the face, but the voice was familiar . . . it seemed to have been gathered into lengths and waves, caught by condensers, then projected into a million loud speakers as the Voice of the News. "The name's Enright. X.B.C. Glad to find you looking fit."

"Thank you," Edward said. He came down slowly, taking care not to let his irritability show on the surface; nevertheless, it ground its heels into his self-control.

"Fine old house," Enright said, glancing around with a show of appreciation. "Throwback to the Neanderthal but a fine old museum piece at that. How many rooms? Forty? Fifty?"

"I have no idea."

"Mind if I look around?"

"Very much."

With a gesture . . . pre-emptory rather than hospitable . . . Edward invited the newscaster to follow him.

The pantry door was open. Edward looked into the kitchen. At least a dozen men were having breakfast. Coffee bubbled and creamed over on the stove. Bacon crimped and snapped in skillets. There were plates heaped with doughnuts within reach of lip-smacking dunkers. And Mrs. Littlefield, for the first time in her life disheveled, was stirring instant pancake mix and eggs into a large crockery bowl. Half-consumed cigarettes smoked in odd dishes or scorched the linoleum on the floor.

Edward paused for a moment. A tangle of cameras, cords, cables and microphones told him who these men were and what they wanted. He heard Enright say: "You can thank Megan Donahue for this." Then he saw her tossing pancakes, putting the spheres into orbit, catching them again to flip them out of the hot butter with a long-handled spatula. Murphy was beside her, waiting for a handout. But when the big dog became aware of Edward he rushed at him with such rapturous force that he sent him staggering back against Enright.

"Megan's dog," the newscaster said. "He seems to know you."

"He does," Edward said. "He slept with me last night."

With Edward's appearance, the kitchen went suddenly silent; like a motion picture stopped in the middle of violent action, the scene froze.

"Go right ahead," Edward said, detaching himself from the dog. The girl turned to him with one of her "white" smiles. "Coffee, sir?"

"Why, yes. Thank you."

Edward took the chair she placed for him at the cluttered table. He glanced at Mrs. Littlefield, expecting some sort of explanation, but she lowered her eyes; she seemed to enjoy the splashes of egg-y mix on her usually spotless apron; lifting a bony hand to brush back a strand of hair, she left a smudge on her cheek, and somehow this simple imperfection gave her a wildly ribald look. And God bless her, Edward thought, her ears are red . . . unlike those oyster-white, old woman's ears with their long, flabby lobes . . . now rosy as a girl's!

"Here's your coffee," Megan said. He saw her smooth forearm and a small grubby hand. "I suppose you're wondering about all this?"

He shook his head. "No. Only I didn't expect to see *you* so soon . . ."

"That only goes to show," she said, "that you have no imagination. Last night I asked your sister to drop me off in the village and here I am."

"I see. This is very good coffee."

Elbows on the table, she leaned down to look sideways into his face. She was wearing the knee-length red sweater,

35

the tight trousers, the lopsided sneakers. Yet she had a morning-scrubbed look, as if she had used soap on her cheeks to polish them. The coffee spilled over into the saucer and as Edward poured the steaming liquid back into the cup he smiled because he knew that she had planned it this way. The cameras were on them now . . . cold eyes that probed for the sensational. One man, squatting, shot the scene from floor level. "Thank you, sir. Thank you very much."

"Not at all," Edward said. His response was agreeable enough, but there could be no doubt that he was annoyed; a sharp stab of anger made him flush and this embarrassed him as it always did.

"I still don't understand," he began, "how these men . . ."

"The gate was open," the girl said. "No one stopped them. They thought they were welcome. They'd been driving all night. They were cold and wet. I thought it would be . . . polite . . . to give them breakfast."

"Of course."

"We all chipped in," she said, "at the store in the village. They won't stay long. They just wanted to be sure that you're . . ."

"I'm what?"

"Well. You are, aren't you?"

"Quite well. Yes."

"Tell them to get their pictures, and they'll go."

"I hope so," Edward said. "I came up here to avoid this sort of thing."

"You should have known better," she said.

There was a pulsing on-and-off of flash bulbs and Edward had a sort of psychic preview of tomorrow's newspapers: a full-page report . . . with pictures . . . of a "public idol" on leave of absence at his "palatial estate" in the North. *And who was the girl?*

36

The rain had stopped. The sun appeared behind a veil of cold mist. Edward glanced at the wall clock; it was just past eight, the hour when Valerie and the boys had always joined him for breakfast. The daily ritual never varied: Valerie believed in punctuality. And in good behavior. Calm, shining like the morning sun, she saw to it that her "men" were properly nourished. The boys turned to her for discipline and were perhaps a little in awe of her because she was always right and always just. Edward was the holiday parent, available only when duty let him off the leash for a few hours and he could ride with them or play catch, or teach them to swim. A year ago, the family had spent a fortnight here at Easterly, most of it swimming or sailing on the lake. It was early in August. Hot and dry and blazingly bright. Edward thought now of the four smooth, strong bodies thrashing in the water, and how it felt to let one of the boys ride his back as if he were a dolphin . . . the small fingers in his hair, the young voice shrill as a fife. His sons had never called him Dad or Pop or Daddy . . . to them, he was Father, and this was Valerie's doing. She said: "You're far too impressive for diminutives, Edward. I couldn't imagine calling you Ed or Eddie!"

Now he put his empty cup down and got to his feet. The newsmen and photographers were clearing their plates of the last crumbs, some of them standing, others perched on the "island" in the middle of the kitchen. There were a few familiar faces; the older men had covered the Washington scene for many years, and had become so much a part of it that they rated no attention ,. . . a bored lot, disillusioned, unimpressed by Preferment or Power. The young men had a sort of jaunty impudence about them, a knowing look, as if there were no secret graves they hadn't already uncovered . . . it was the evidence only which they pursued along the

37

corridors of Government, racing like hungry wolves through forests of microphones along cold marble floors. The fleeing victims were the current V.I.P.'s . . . notoriety being more tasty, as far as the pack was concerned, than accomplishment.

Edward decided to control his temper and to make at least a show of good nature.

"The sun's out," he said. "You're welcome to take as many pictures as you like. Not indoors. I'm sorry. But at the moment . . ."

"Okay. Outside."

There was a general stir of departure, a gathering up of equipment, a last gulp of coffee. Edward sensed that the mood wasn't hostile or resentful. It crossed his mind that the girl might have conditioned these men somehow; at least she had fed them! And he recalled the sound of laughter . . . the unfamiliar sound that had wakened him from heavy, exhausted sleep. He recalled, too, that all night his hand must have been closed upon the "feeling" of a revolver; he had found his fingers stiffened into that position, so that it was hard to open them.

Enright, whom Edward had found warming himself before the fire in the hallway, wasn't as easily shaken off as the others. He wanted a "statement," he said.

"About what?"

"Why the secrecy? Why *here*, exactly? Why alone? How about your staff? *They* didn't seem to know. Why . . ."

"Under the circumstances," Edward interrupted, "no statement is necessary."

"Oh, I understand, of course," Enright interrupted. "A shocking experience . . . Please believe that I'm most sympathetic . . ."

"Thank you," Edward interrupted. "You have your story."

38

"How long will you be here?"

"I don't know." Edward turned abruptly away. *Damn it,* he thought. *Damn it. Damn it.*

Murphy followed him through the pantry and across the dining-room to the hallway. Edward let both doors swing shut with a resounding *whoosh*, as if he had kicked them . . . Murphy wasn't a disciplined dog. Edward knew that if he sat down, he would be licked again . . . not too comfortable for the dog considering the raspy condition of Edward's face . . . and so he added a log to the fire and tried to warm himself. It wasn't often that he shivered, but he was shivering now.

He expected the girl to follow him, as Murphy had, but he hoped not for the same reasons.

"May I sit down?" she asked, and added: "Sir?"

Edward nodded toward a chair and for a moment she sat primly, then curled herself up like an anchovy on a slice of toast, leaving her disreputable sneakers on the floor beside her. Edward thought he had never seen a more forlorn creature, only there was nothing forlorn about her eyes. Her hair was tangled as if it had never known a brush. How old was she? Hard to say. Not young, now that he really looked at her. Thirty, perhaps. Certainly not pampered. Her hands . . small, well-shaped . . . were rough . . . But then . . . He put up his fingers and rubbed his chin with the rueful conviction that he was no prize, himself . . .

"You're divine unshaven," she said. "A god down from Olympus for a look around! What do you think of us?"

Edward let this pass. He had a way of making people talk, simply by towering over them and staring beyond them as if they didn't exist for him; this created in others the most overpowering need to explain themselves, to make themselves understood. He did this now.

39

"I suppose you want to know why I ran out on your sister," the girl said. "I knew why she turned suddenly gracious and whisked me away wearing her fur coat. She had noticed my charm. She had no intention of leaving me here with you. Am I right? Am I right, sir?"

"I dare say you are."

"As we drove through the village I noticed a light in the motel where I stayed last summer. I got out there, and left the coat and said goodnight to your sister. She drove off. She had to. But you should have seen her face! The motel people remembered me and put me up. This morning before dawn the Press arrived. They won't bother you again. There's nothing newsworthy about a good-natured man in need of a shave who shares his breakfast with the boys." She broke off. "I suppose you're wondering about yesterday?"

"You met that fellow in a bar you said. Begin from there."

"Him? Oh! Him.

She was silent for a moment, running her fingers through her hair and dragging it down in straggling points across her forehead so that she looked not like an otter or a cat or an anchovy but like a Cairn terrier.

Finally she said: "I was walking Murphy. I live in an awful room near the Square and Murphy's locked up most of the time while I'm out scouting for news. You see, I write a sort of gossip column for a trade paper . . . the garment trade. For peanuts. I went into this bar because Murphy's welcome there. He hides under a table. I don't drink but I like coffee. And this fellow was there. From a rival paper. A sort of free-lancer. He said 'Hi' and asked if I'd heard you had disappeared. I hadn't but I thought: he's at Easterly, of course. I remembered seeing you up here last summer. I used to watch you and your family. I'd watch for hours. You know . . . Cinderella. The Prince. I'd be on the beach, turning hot and cold and sighing like a furnace and dreaming how you'd notice me and the next thing I knew I'd be in the White House and Piatagorsky would be playing a waltz and I'd be dancing with you . . . So I promised the guy I'd get him into Easterly if he'd drive me up . . . I knew all about the road along the lake and the path up to the house. We didn't stop to pack as much as a comb! But he brought along a bottle. He drove into that ditch because he was too drunk to avoid it. Not that I cared. Not for myself. But when Murphy swam ashore and disappeared . . ."

She held out her hand and the big dog moved away from Edward's side and went to her.

"He likes you," she said. And then glancing up at Edward she said: "I think you ought to keep him. He's had his shots. He's really a country dog . . . He loathes Washington Square and all those filthy pigeons and sparrows."

"I couldn't," Edward said. "I'm sorry."

"I think you need him," she insisted. "When you were on the dock yesterday you didn't see me at first. I thought you looked . . . alone."

She uncurled and stood up feeling with dirty bare toes for the sneakers.

"You could take him for collateral," she said.

"Collateral?"

"I'm stone broke. I'll have to pay the motel for last night's lodging. And my room rent when I get back to New York. And I haven't a cent."

"Who's going to drive you home?"

"Enright. He's waiting. Could you? Could you let me have fifty dollars if I leave Murphy?"

"I suppose so. Wait here. My wallet's upstairs."

Edward went to his room and came back with a hundred dollars.

"Murphy's worth it," he said, putting the money into the girl's hand and folding her fingers over it. "You can claim him whenever you like . . ."

She might have been about to thank him, but before she could, the telephone in the library rang. Edward reacted from long habit to the sound of that particular bell. He excused himself and went quickly to answer.

The familiar voice, sympathetic but not concerned, at least not on the surface: "I think you did the right thing, leaving the hospital. Only remember certain decisions can't wait too long. The blueprint, excellent as it is, isn't quite enough. Proving the validity of the plan . . . its strength and its final value, lies ahead and it's all yours. *What* you build has got to be strong, and *final*. You're needed here. You know that. But don't come back until you're ready for the fight of your life."

Edward wanted to say that he was ready now. He hesitated because once more the thought of responsibility made his heart pound. The damnable pain began to throb and hammer inside his head. He stammered something unintelligible and the dry voice cut in with cautious platitudes: "Take care of yourself. Let me know if there's anything . . ."

Edward hung up. He stood for a moment with his fingers pressed hard against his closed eyes. Behind them, he thought, was his brain: elaborate convolutions of gray matter . . . the computer . . . into which intelligence fed its findings. Inert and useless substance unless charged with that mysterious force, sanity! Given. Or withheld. Somehow, in the helpless drop from the torn sky, he had lost contact. Or almost. Intermittently, the charge came through, the orders were received, the sum was arrived at . . . and then confusion. All his knowledge of the world, its needs, its perils, the vast, swift changes taking place, were no longer clear, exciting, urgent or even real. He could abandon his great opportunities for service and not concern himself with the result, or grieve for lost prestige. It was as if a poison-tipped shaft . . . futility

42

. . . had struck deep into the computer-brain, cutting off ambition.

He went slowly back to the hallway. The girl was gone. But Murphy, splendidly aware of his new position as head dog in this man's house, waited like a black statue, one paw raised as if he had flushed a pheasant.

Then Edward realized that he didn't know anything, really, about Megan Donahue. He went to the entrance door and looked out. A fleet of cars maneuvered the wide turn and charged down the driveway toward the gate. Megan was in one of them . . . which one Edward couldn't even guess.

Toward noon, Eithne called: "Have you seen the papers? Surprisingly conservative coverage, so far . . . And by the way what became of that dreadful girl?"

Edward pulled himself with difficulty out of a sudden sense of letdown. "I have no idea," he said.

"Good. Keep it that way! She's a meddling tramp. I warned you, remember! How do you feel?"

Then, without waiting for an answer, she told him that she had caught up with Ricardo in Milan. He was on his way and would fly straight to Easterly. "Perhaps he can strip off that mask you're wearing and *have* worn ever since the accident. It frightens me, Edward."

"It needn't," he said. As he hung up, he thought he'd better go outside and walk, and never mind shaving; what had that girl said about his being divine with a blue chin?

"Murphy," he asked, "how about a walk?"

Murphy searched anxiously for something he missed. "No leashes here," Edward said. "This is country. These are the great open spaces. Let's go."

The big dog almost knocked him down on the threshold, and once free on the brown lawn ran in circles, cutting out wedges of sod with his sharp, untrimmed city claws. Edward thought he'd keep away from the beach. He could hear the labored efforts of a tow car from the village as it hauled out the wreck. Better go the other way, down the slope to the stables. Have a look at the old Rolls . . . *Forget. Forget. Forget* . . .

The stalls had been cleaned but there were still shreds of straw on the floor, drifts of golden dust in the corners and clinging to old spiders' webs that swung like nets from beam to beam overhead. Although there was no wind outside, here in this big, echoing place it was drafty and cold. The bins, where the saddle horses used to blow and nibble at their feed, contained nothing more than a few grains of brown oats and the dessicated remnants of last summer's grasshoppers trapped by the smooth sides of their prison.

Murphy explored the stalls, making contact with a reality he had almost, but not quite, abjured. He didn't wag; rather, his tail quivered from root to tip, and his nose rotated, dripping with sensuous delight in animal smells, the delicious ammonia smells that meant: "Horses have been here." Edward wondered what the big dog's beginnings had been . . . where did he come from and how had he fallen upon lean days with a city girl who led him along pavements by a leash and trained him to wait under tables in bars, supine, exhausted by broken dreams and hopeless yearnings? Had he ever been mated? Probably not. Into what corner of his being had he thrust his longing for love? Was that the word? Yes. Love. There was no other. Edward had seen it happen: the proud, strong male dog indifferent for once to the master man, disobedient if he must be, caught into an unfamiliar splendor. Edward had watched such a courtship . . . the moment of recognition: *This is she. This is my beloved.* And the exquisite moments of preparation. Rollicking play and joyous chases, until their thudding hearts forced them to lie,

44

facing one another, paws extended, muzzles down, eyes calm and deep, waiting for the next step in the ritual . . . the fulfillment, the triumph, the sense-command obeyed, its purpose completed.

Edward thought that if he kept Murphy he would buy a female retriever and when puppies came, keep them, too, until they were old enough to give to children who could prove that they were capable of raising them. This was something he had intended to teach his sons: respect, as Schweitzer said, for all life. Life, the learning time! No wonder men spent so much of it trying to stay alive, knowing all the while that they wouldn't, couldn't . . . There was always the unforseen trap, the stumble, the fall, the inevitable blackout. But in the beginning, what miracles, what delights!

And Edward thought of his own youth, time of challenge, when the future was like space, to be entered because it was there, shimmering with star dust, hung with immense unknowable spheres, beautiful yet hostile, perhaps the answer.

He went on into the tack room. A few old bridles and rusted bits had been left when the place was dismantled and some framed snapshots still hung on the wall above the desk. There was one of Valerie riding Fucile. Clenching his hands, Edward forced himself to look at it. Pearl-blonde, not yet twenty when the picture was taken, slim and straight, unsmiling, concentrating on the business at hand. Where was the ribbon Valerie had won *that* day? So many ribbons! Had she really valued them or, taking her own horsemanship for granted, had she tossed them aside?

Edward remembered the first time he saw her. A match for him, shoulder high to his height, classically beautiful, a sort of counterpoint to his own spectacular ugliness. He first became aware of her at a State dinner in Washington. A bank of flowers separated them but whenever she glanced at Edward he saw the reflected sparks of candlelight in her eyes and felt as if she had touched a taper to his dry heart, setting it afire. The sudden blaze of feeling turned him faint. The women at his right and left decided that his charm had been overrated ; he was both rude and dull. For once, he didn't care. He was in love. If that was a reversal to a dated sentimentality, then so be it! He watched Valerie, letting himself imagine a different seating arrangement: himself at the head of this table, Valerie at its foot. If it should happen . . . if some day he should occupy that chair . . . Valerie was the woman he'd want near at hand . . . a wife who would always do, say, think the right thing. He had had affairs but with women who had failed, not him but themselves. He had been disappointed too often not to have become critical. But he thought of loving Valerie as a parched man thinks of drinking at a spring of clear water.

The drinking, when at last he reached the spring, did nothing to quench his thirst.

There had been a brief honeymoon and then Edward took up his duties again. Valerie went wherever he did, gracious, calm, as if conditioned by a lifetime of exposure to "public" life, although until she married Edward she had lived with her grandmother in Charleston. He sometimes wondered whether it was his position, not his ideals, that made her match every forward step he took. She gave him a promissory note but offered him no security.

The first time she was pregnant she left him and went back to Charleston for the final months. "They say romantic love dies on the delivery table," she said. "I don't want you to see me like this! In another week I'll look like a Yankee clipper under full sail!" And with one of her faint smiles: "You stay away, Edward, until it's over. I'll let you know when I'm fit

46

to be seen again. Like this, we keep the illusion . . ."

"Illusion?"

"You didn't marry me for my wit, did you?"

He let her have her way and David was four months old when Edward flew back from Europe and held his first-born in his arms. He found Valerie as immaculate, as unruffled, as slim as ever . . . twenty-two now and willing to lie with him in the secret dark, taking no delight in his own strong and healthy body, returning his kisses with lips that had been instructed, but hadn't learned their lesson.

Edward whistled to Murphy and went outside. The sun had defeated the mist; there was warmth in it now; an imaginative poet could have sensed a sort of stirring in the soil where the hibernating seeds made ready to climb toward the surface. Soon there would be a blush of green over the fields; the compost heaps would steam under the thrust of the prodding forks, and birds . . . a few at a time . . . would fly in from the South. Murphy ran ahead, pausing every now and then to look back at Edward, worried perhaps that this blissful belonging might not be real. Reassured, he took off again, and Edward followed, walking miles farther than he had intended, so that it was dark before he got back to Easterly, and waited there for Ricardo.

A cool dawn grayed the library windows, but indoors it was warm and bright.

Ricardo said: "I was in Milan when Eithne called . . . a brief stopover on my way home. I had only to change my flight reservations, move them forward a few days. You see, at times I throw my weight around! I had no trouble at all; they made room for me and my secretary on a jet and before we had had time to fasten our seat belts we were in Boston. Boston to Portland and then by helicopter to your field . . ."

47

He broke off. "It needs attention by the way."

"I don't doubt it," Edward said.

They were relaxed in the old velvet chairs. Coffee steamed on a "hot table" Edward had wheeled in from the kitchen. "An anachronism in such a house as this," Ricardo said, glancing around the room. "Have you no servants, Edward?"

"A caretaker and his wife do what's necessary. They'll be along at eight. Then we'll have breakfast."

The two men regarded each other with the affectionate appreciation of old friends. Ricardo wasn't as tall as Edward remembered nor by any means as young. His hair had turned from pepper to salt, close-cut yet coarse and somehow shaggy. The shock of this change and a whole new complex of wrinkles set Edward back on his heels for a moment, but soon he saw the Ricardo he knew behind the unimportant differences. And there was still the magnificent "cello" voice with none of the nasal singsong of the altar and the pulpit. He was dressed informally in severe black and might have been any obscure parish priest. His handsome head against the chair-back, he stretched his legs and Edward noticed his well-shod feet. There was the subdued glint of a crucifix but no other indication of his exalted rank. . .

"It was good of you to come," Edward said. "Eithne shouldn't have asked you to, but I'm glad she did."

"I would have come as quickly twenty years ago," Ricardo said. And with an unexpected twinkle he added: "But I think I knew, even then, that we were both destined to be Very Important People."

Edward shook his head. "Are we? I suppose so. I wish I might have been there when you received the hat. Your letters caught up with me a month later. You made the consistory seem very real! Only you didn't say what your feelings were."

"I could hear my heart pounding," Ricardo admitted. "Bang! Bang! Like a drum!"

"What did you think of?"

"Nothing. Nothing beyond my own dignity . . . not to faint or stammer or forget. Later, I had all the reactions . . . but delayed. I remember being exultant and humble and grateful. Not many men are so honored in their lifetime."

"Have you ever wished that you could relive the war years?"

"Oh, yes. But I'd like to correct certain memories. Lie a little. Pretend that I wasn't driven by the most unchristian hate most of the time."

Ricardo seemed to look into the past; instinctively, he touched the crucifix as if making contact with a spiritual force, re-charging himself through the tips of his fingers.

"I slogged my way up the Boot with our infantry," he said finally, "and did what I could for the wounded and the dying. Often I was too late. I could have been ten priests and still couldn't have reached them all."

"But youth," Edward insisted. "Have you let go of it without a struggle?"

"Not entirely . . . And you?"

"I'd enjoy being with my squadron again," Edward admitted. "A brotherhood of effort. An *esprit de corps* impossible in civilian life. We risked our necks, but not for medals. I wonder, was it the last of chivalry? A bunch of drunken brawlers at midnight, a company of cold-sober fliers at dawn! It's true it was a war without a slogan. But one thing I can swear to; there was a built-in purpose . . . a *reason* for risking our necks . . . I didn't imagine it. It wasn't mentioned, but it was there. I'd like to feel like that again."

"Don't you?" Ricardo asked with a note of surprise in his voice.

49

Edward shook his head. "I reason, nowadays; I don't feel."

He broke off with a flush of embarrassment. "That sounds like self-pity, doesn't it?"

"Perhaps it is . . . Let's have a look at it. Your being here. What does it mean, exactly?"

"I don't know," Edward said. "What did Eithne tell you?"

"Enough to trouble me deeply." Ricardo's eyes sharpended suddenly. "You *look* well. Why then, those weeks in the hospital? Were you injured? Is what ails you physical?" And when Edward shook his head, Ricardo went on to say that Eithne seemed to believe that the damage was mental. "But I see no evidence of that!"

"What evidence would there be?" Edward demanded with a twinge of anger. "Did you expect to find me slobbering like an idiot?"

"You've been through enough to have toppled a steadier mind than yours," Ricardo said. He held out his cup, and when Edward had refilled it, stirred the steaming brew until he had reduced it to the right temperature. Then he said quietly: "I've watched you through the years. There's a soaring idealism in everything you undertake that marks you as a leader evoked by the world's need. Great men seem to appear rarely. They flash in the darkness, as you have once or twice. I have great faith in you, Edward. But there's no time to lose. I ask you again: What are you doing here?"

Edward went to the window. Murphy, who had been lying at his feet, got up and followed.

After a moment Edward said: "When I killed Valerie and my sons, I killed my future. I can't make myself believe that there's any reason to go on. I simply don't care."

"Your saying so," Ricardo interrupted, "proves that you do."

50

Edward turned away from the window and came back to face his friend again.

"Last night," he said, "waiting for you to come, I tried to reassemble my shattered purpose. I really tried, Ricardo. But somehow the fragments wouldn't fit together. The American dream. A way to define it. Then to achieve it. Had I ever known? Had I ever even remotely guessed? What a fatuous ass I've been to think I might help to save these millions of people from failure . . ."

"We advance step by step . . ."

"I sat in the dark," Edward interrupted, "and God, it was quiet! I tried to recall the Plan. What's been accomplished. What still has to be done. The details kept slipping away, disappearing . . . a nightmare of confusion. There'd be a flash of realization, then a mind-full of fragments. The conviction that I was helpless took hold. A complete aloneness. Then I heard the helicopter. I knew it was bringing you and that if I didn't get to you soon it would be too late. I rushed out of the house and ran all the way to the field. Certain sounds trigger the panic. It was those blades clacking up there in the dark! And then that great hovering thing set down and the fear drained out of me like blood out of a wound and I thought: Ricardo will tell me what to do."

Ricardo said nothing. He put the empty cup aside and clasped his hands, staring down at his ring with a curious, fixed concentration. Edward thought how much he looked the Cardinal he had recently become, and wondered whether the calling shapes the man, as artists in some mysterious way influence the landscape they paint so that Japanese trees turn into Hokusais and French fields into Van Goghs and sunsets into Turners. The muscular-minded, reckless soldier-priest Edward had known in Italy had become the tempered aristocrat. Ricardo's face had lost its young radiance; it was the face, now, of a man who has learned caution. And yet when he looked up, Edward saw in his eyes the compassion he needed. He was grateful that it wasn't condemnation he saw there.

"Eithne was wrong," Ricardo said. "Your trouble isn't insanity or anything like it. You anticipate what I'm going to call it and will reject my diagnosis."

"How do you know I will?"

Ricardo spread out his hands. "You'll reject it because it will frighten you. Like telling an apparently healthy man that he has cancer. I'm going to ask you to step away from yourself and then from a little distance to look back at what you are."

Edward smiled. "All right. What am I?"

"A knight riding full tilt to the rescue of Man."

"I've never had any other purpose!"

"But you have no lance! How do you expect to bring the enemy down, unarmed as you are?"

"You mean God."

"I mean God. Believe me, Edward, I'm as troubled as you are by Man's predicament: crushed by the exploding masses, cheated by the machine, confronted by the fact of the bomb and the enigma of space. I watch the trees fall and the bulldozers clawing at the soil and the rivers and streams boiling with poisonous detergents and I weep . . . Only when I pray can I clear my soul of rebellion."

There was a pause, and then Ricardo said: "I've prayed for *you*, Edward." His voice tightened, the cello sounding a note up the scale. "I dare say you expect results? An immediate answer? Examine your thoughts! Isn't the relief you seek already there? Or are you attached to this fear? Are you an invalid relishing his illness?"

"The doctors have hinted as much. But what do you

52

expect? They're realists. They have no idea how to suture a torn conscience. They hear a jangle of off-key bells inside a man's skull and tell him he's psychosomatic and to go home and be a good boy and take aspirin and get plenty of sleep. Or else they point to a shadow on an X-ray transparency and say 'tumor' and cut the shadow out. They found no such shadow in my case. My legs jump when my knees are tapped. My kidney tests are negative. My heart races too fast, but that's shock. My eyes see. My blood pressure's normal . . ."

Edward shouted suddenly: "And so I got the hell out of their laboratory . . . as animals cannot, except by willing their own deaths!"

"So that's it," Ricardo said, his eyes deepening suddenly. "Are you leading me toward the truth about yourself? Are you willing your own death? You say certain sounds trigger it. Trigger what? Tell me, if you can."

"It begins like a presentiment." Edward searched for the right words. "Something reminds me of the accident and against my will I relive it. And then despair takes hold. And finally intention: pin pointed: do it, somehow! But do it! And I will, unless you can tell me how to unlock the cage I'm in."

"The key," Ricardo said after a moment, "is faith. Accept it, or stay in your cage."

He looked up at Edward with a smile. "If you were a Catholic like your sister," he said, "you would know this. But haven't you always resisted God? Doubted Him? I do not. I am sure. But to convince *you*! In a few minutes! I tried, many years ago, do you remember? And I failed."

Ricardo leaned back and closed his eyes. Edward thought that he might have fallen asleep, and he was waiting quietly to make sure when Mrs. Littlefield came in. "We heard the helicopter," she said, "so we're here earlier than usual. The sun's just up. I see you've had coffee."

Edward glanced at Ricardo. "My friend's asleep. He flew all the way from Italy to have breakfast with me. He'll be hungry when he wakes."

"I could fix bacon and eggs," she said. She glanced at Ricardo doubtfully; she had caught the gleam of the crucifix against the black of his garment. And opening his eyes suddenly he said, "Not bacon and eggs! Something native. Codfish cakes or blueberry muffins . . ."

Mrs. Littlefield frowned. Was this a Catholic gentleman? Probably. And steeling herself against prejudice she said: "It's too early for blueberries."

"Mrs. Littlefield," Edward interrupted, "this is Ricardo Cardinal Drury."

She acknowledged the introduction with a twitch of her head but avoided the unfamiliar title as if it might scratch her Episcopalian tongue. She could never have brought herself to call a man of the cloth "Father."

"I could heat up last night's fish chowder, Mr. Drury," she said.

"Good." Ricardo turned to Edward. "You see, once many years ago, I spent an autumn in this state of yours. I've never forgotten the pumpkin pies and the spiced apples and the piccalilli relish and the brown bread . . . Those were the good old days!"

Mrs. Littlefield bridled, but proudly. "Things don't change in these parts," she said.

She wheeled the table back to the kitchen, china and silverware rattling and tinkling from rug to rug along the hall. And presently a smell of chowder drifted through the house. Murphy rose from his place at Edward's feet and went to snuffle at the pantry door.

54

After breakfast Edward suggested a drive. He had spent the previous afternoon helping the Rolls descend from the jacks. It had landed on its feet, had shaken itself, shuddered, and was as ready as ever to take off.

Ricardo found the old car adorable: a *Ninon de L'Enclos* of a machine, he called it, ageless, beguiling! "I own a Ferrari, myself. I don't use it here in America. But when I'm in Italy I drive at high speeds along the new autostrade, feeling very young and reckless."

"You'll never be old."

"I was born old," Ricardo protested. "That's why it was no shock to turn seventy. How old are *you*, Edward? I admit I've forgotten, if I ever knew."

Edward hesitated. Then with a smile he said: "Younger men are beginning to patronize me."

"Not you!" Ricardo shouted. "They wouldn't dare. Fame and accomplishment are guarantees against that sort of thing. Who would have patronized Churchill in his nineties? Who would have presumed to patronize Berenson or Toscanini? Only lazy nobodies let the young take over. Age is *their* alibi. Don't let it be yours!"

They had circled the Easterly property and for a mile or two rolled majestically along an unpaved road, then parked on a wooded promontory overlooking the lake. The air was soft and warm, the sky cloudless. Far out on the silver-blue sheet of water small gusts of wind blew triangles of darker blue, steel-blue . . . a lonely, distant ruffling, like the panic-stricken flight of small fish. In shore, the ripples broke with little soft slaps. Five deer crossed in front of the car, their tails flickering as they disappeared into a ravine. For a moment it was all Edward could do to keep Murphy from jumping out of the window. Now was the time to prove who was master. The struggle was brief but final and with a quick lick at Edward's restraining hand Murphy lay down again.

But for a long time he trembled.

"How beautiful it is," Ricardo said. "I don't wonder you've never sold it. I suppose you should."

"Why?"

"You know quite well why. A place like this is a luxury. Turn it into cash and give the cash to the poor."

"You can say that? You and your palaces, your jewels, your churches?"

"They belong to everyone, Edward. But this . . ." Ricardo made an expansive gesture. "Who sees it? Who uses it?"

Edward said nothing. He thought that Easterly would have belonged, in time, to his sons. Now the line was broken, since Eithne was childless. Soon the property would deteriorate, unless he, himself, lived here. Cultivated his acres. Waited for the end. Or found the courage to hasten it. Nothing that Ricardo had said had helped at all. Accept God. Give of your substance. Have faith. How? Ricardo hadn't felt the bodies of a wife and sons turn cold beneath frantic kisses, freeze into death and silence. He hadn't known the darkest depths of guilt. He was blameless. He had never killed. *Ricardo had never killed.*

Suddenly Ricardo put his hand on Edward's arm.

"What will you do now?" he asked. "I can't stay here watching every move you make for fear you'll kill yourself."

"I wouldn't want that," Edward said. "It would be the library lamp all over again."

Ricardo gave him a startled look, but Edward didn't explain.

"You've played an important role in two administrations," Ricardo went on after a moment. "I've heard it said that you're in line for the Presidency. I think I've known this since the day I met you. Others know it; there's an aura of greatness about you. And yet you have this maggot in your brain: suicide! Let's stop beating about the bush. Let's name it . . . Forrestal, Hemingway. Now you? A splatter of blood defacing your life's work? Why? Because, like them, you're afraid that you've stopped functioning?"

Ricardo leaned forward and touched the instrument panel. "This car has been standing idle for years, you say. All it needed was a spark, a little push forward. It runs."

"Someday it will stop for good."

"Yes. When it's supposed to."

"Fatalism?" Edward demanded.

Ricardo answered quietly: "I prefer to call it Divine Decision. Can't you let it go at that and not try to force the issue? Why not live life, not fight it?"

"I'm asking *you*," Edward said with a smile. "You're supposed to have all the answers!"

It was Ricardo's turn to feel a twinge of anger.

"Forgive me," Edward said quickly. "It's not that I don't want to live out my span. I'm afraid to."

"Why? You're well on your way to becoming an American image. Is that the word? I think so. One of the Faces every school child learns to recognize and to remember. It's your duty to keep the image undefiled. Who can look at a picture of Mussolini without seeing superimposed that horror dripping with spittal swinging upside down from a Milanese lamp post? And Hitler. In spite of the superman pose, the fiery eyes, the *swastika*, isn't there always the final scene in the bunker, the stain on the sofa? But consider such men as Roosevelt dragging his useless legs from decision to decision . . . Wilson pleading for the League with the last of his voice . . . No suicides here! I wouldn't be surprised if Kennedy weren't someday to be one of the galaxy. It took an assassin's bullets to bring him down, but he would never have fired those shots himself!"

Ricardo turned toward Edward and they looked at each other steadily for a moment. Then, Ricardo said: "You're

57

aware, aren't you, that I haven't used the word cowardice? I
don't believe you're a coward, but if you are, you can handle
it. And that's bravery."

He gave Edward a quick look. "You've said nothing about
this to anyone else?"

"Nothing."

"Don't. It's the wedge that could split the work you're
doing and bring it down."

He glanced at Edward's wrist. "Eleven-thirty. Take me
back to the field, please. The helicopter's picking me up at
noon. I left my secretary in Portland explaining my change of
plans and setting up appointments in New Orleans for
tomorrow. I must be on my way."

At the field, waiting in the warm sunlight, Ricardo said
that if Edward were to let go of Easterly his concern for Man
might carry more weight. Yet he thought it unlikely that
Edward would give away his millions and live in a jungle or a
slum, or that he, himself, would retreat to a hermit's cave and
preach to the owls and bats!

"I admit, I'm a devout worldling! Good music. Fine
buildings. Texture and polish. The weight and breathing
reality of great sculpture. Art and thought and superior
behavior down through the ages delight me and always will.
But beyond these testimonials of human progress, there is the
guarantee of immortality: the persistence of good. This
sustains me in my service. As it will you, Edward. Believe!
You must. Otherwise my coming here today will have
accomplished nothing."

Edward had always resented instruction; he had to find
things out for himself. Yet he admitted that the infernal
headache had let go. "I'm not shaking inside and blowing
with every gust of thought like an old newspaper whipped
along the streets. But how long will it last? And if it starts

58

again tonight when I'm alone, can I stop it?"

"Go back to your work," Ricardo said sharply. "Go back today. You won't be alone."

When the helicopter had lifted from the field, had hovered and turned and drifted away like a great benign dragonfly, Edward drove the Rolls back to the garage, ran to the house and took the stairs up to his room two at a time. Murphy thought this was a game and nipped joyously at his master's flying heels.

The last thing Ricardo had said was that he'd be seeing Edward in Washington in a few days. "We'll talk again." And seated in the soaring bubble he had lifted his hand and with a smile had evoked the mystic blessing.

3

Edward had brought only one suitcase to Easterly. He began now to pack it. He felt a strong excitement, something feverish, not quite healthy. Emptying the bureau drawers of his few things he stuffed them into the suitcase; his toilet articles followed. Then, snapping the lid shut, he went to the closet for his coat. The wrong closet because the coat wasn't there. Instead several women's dresses swung from hangers, while a pair of high-heeled white slippers stood pigeon-toed on the floor as if the wearer had just stepped out of them.

The realization that these things had belonged to Valerie came instantly. The fragrance of a flowery perfume she had always used was faint and disembodied; a ghost of lost sweetness. The dresses still bore the imprint of her body . . . the swell of her small breasts, the curve-in of her waist. Yet they bore, too, evidence of the laundress' iron; every plait was pressed flat. He had been careful when Valerie was alive not to "muss" her neatness. She always bent forward to him, offering her cheek, never leaning against him unless he forced her to. If he happened to disturb the effect when she was dressed for some special occasion, she always ran back to change from head to foot. Not angrily. She was never ill-tempered, only determined to excel. And excel she did! "I want you to be proud of me, Edward."

He thought now that pride in her was at the core of his love for her. He could find nothing to criticize or to alter. Her house, her clothes, her children, her behavior, her voice, the way she entertained were all achievements, arrived at with no apparent effort. She was, besides, one of the most beautiful women in America, a creation renewed day after day, year after year. She was always on guard against any sign of fatigue or illness that might blur the clean, clear contours of her face. Her brow was round, innocent, pure as a child's. Her hair, gold touched with fire, shone like a pampered cat's; she could touch it with a brush and it sprang to the bristles. Her flesh was always cool; there were no warm velvet dimples about her nudity; it had been like holding a young swimmer, the muscles hard beneath the skin, powerful. Powerful in resistence to love. Powerful in giving birth. Strange, this power in so fragile a creature. Edward had seen it in certain ballet dancers. It was a strength deliberately achieved and maintained; there was no room for anything else if a woman possessed it.

Suddenly Edward jerked the dresses down, and carrying the armload over to the bed, dumped everything into a heap. A tangle of shapelessness reminded him . . . But this time, he fought to stem the rising tide of memory. Scooping the things up again he went to the window and would have thrown them out only that he became suddenly aware that he was being watched. He had left the door open and Mrs. Littlefield stood on the threshold. Her expression was cold and suspicious, as if she had discovered him in an act of

62

betrayal. It wasn't the first time in his life that he had had to meet that look, but he had never before deserved it. Ashamed and speechless, he let the armload of dresses fall to the floor.

"I'm sorry. I forgot to clear out that closet," Mrs. Littlefield said. "It's my fault. She left those things last summer and asked me to give them away."

She crossed stiffly to where Edward stood and picked up the crumpled dresses.

"Your coat's in the other closet," she said. And then, noticing the suitcase, she asked if he was leaving. And when he nodded, she asked: "Is it because of what the television people said this morning?"

"I didn't watch television this morning. I was with Cardinal Drury."

"I thought your sister might have called you. She must be very upset."

"About what? Don't be so damned secretive! Is it something I ought to know?"

"One of the men who was here yesterday morning . . . I think his name was Enright . . . talked about you for half an hour."

"That's nothing new," Edward said irritably. "It happens all the time."

Mrs. Littlefield frowned. She began to smooth out the wrinkled dresses, to rearrange them across her arm.

"Well?"

Mrs. Littlefield was embarrassed but she was in for it now and had to stumble through the sorry report:

"He said the doctors back in Washington should have told the truth. Said the American people had a right to know. Someone as high up as you. Said the truth was called for with things in the country as bad as they are now."

"The truth?" Edward demanded. "About what?"

"He didn't say so right out . . . he just hinted that maybe

you aren't . . . quite well since the accident. Mr. Littlefield and I were pretty mad when we heard that. *We* know how you are."

Edward smiled. "How am I?"

"A man you can trust," she said, a sudden tremor in her voice.

Edward shook his head, but he said nothing.

"Maybe you'd better not leave Easterly today," Mrs. Littlefield went on. "I'm not the one to give you adivce. But if you stay out the week, they can't say you care *what* they say . . ."

She went to the door, and paused on the threshold without looking back at him.

"I came upstairs," she said, "to tell you a friend of yours is in the library. His name's Scott. I said you were here. Do you want to see him?"

"Scott?" Edward shouted. "You bet your life I do!"

He brushed past Mrs. Littlefield and took the steps down as fast as he had come up. The game had been interrupted, but it was still a game and Murphy ran ahead, stumbling on the thick stair carpet, barking and wagging, to make the acquaintance of whoever might be in the library. *Company! Hurrah!*

Scott was looking at two small paintings . . . landscapes . . . almost leaning into them he was so absorbed. But when he heard Edward, he swung around and they shook hands.

"I'm glad to see you," Scott said. He seemed to have transferred his interest in the paintings and to be absorbed, now, in Edward's appearance. "I'm on my way to open the studio for the summer. When I heard you were here, I decided to cut across to Easterly and see for myself . . ."

"That television interview?" Edward interrupted. "I'm supposed to have lost my marbles?"

"Oh, nothing that definite," Scott protested. "It was, at

64

most, innuendo. It would have passed right over most people's heads."

"I've learned not to pay attention to anonymous letters and rumor that stops just short of slander," Edward said. "I could sue the network, I suppose, for broadcasting a pack of dirty lies. But I won't. I'd only be giving importance to over-the-fence gossip."

Scott laughed. "I see you're still very much yourself!"

"I hope so."

"How long will you be staying here?"

"I planned to leave today."

"Couldn't you wait over until, say, Monday? You've never seen my studio, have you? I'll drive you up there and on my way back to Lucky River tomorrow, I'll drop you off here. What do you say?"

Edward thought: "Another reprieve." And he felt a lift of gratitude and relief.

Aloud, he said: "I think I'd like that very much, Scott. But there's a catch; I have a dog. I'd have to take him along."

Scott glanced down at Murphy. "This fellow? By all means. I'm driving a station wagon. Plenty of room. What's his name?"

"Murphy."

"From the royal kennels?"

Edward ignored this although he smiled at Scott's impudence.

While Edward went to tell Mrs. Littlefield that he had taken her advice and wouldn't be going to Washington after all, Scott must have returned to his scrutiny of the two old paintings, because he was looking at them when Edward came back.

"Shurtleff and Gifford," he said and almost smacked his

65

lips. "If you ever think of selling them, let me know, won't you?"

"I'll give them to you."

"But you'll miss them, won't you?"

"Of course. There's no point in giving away something you yourself don't value."

Scott nodded. "That's true. But I'm afraid I'm not that generous. Just let anyone try to get these two marvels away from *me*! Look at this Gifford . . . painted in 1897 at Nonquit. That's Buzzard's Bay country. There's almost nothing left of the place Gifford knew." Scott took the canvas down and held it at arm's length. "Notice the rocks in the meadow . . . they're still warm from the noontime sun. How crisp the lichen is! And that boiling up of clouds heavy with thunder. God, how Gifford must have loved New England, and how he could paint it! He's given us the smell of that particular spot! here. Hold it."

Edward held the painting while Scott lifted the Shurtleff from its hook. Edward thought that Mrs. Littlefield was one housekeeper in a million; there wasn't a trace of dust on the ornate gold frame. He suffered a pang of shame because he had never really looked at the canvasses, or if he had looked at them it was with eyes cheated by the familiar. He saw now that Shurtleff had painted a forest. Shafts of sunlight slanted from the tops of the trees like transparent pillars. It was easy to imagine a dance of deer flies in the misty radiance.

"This must be Keene Valley," Scott said. "Sixty years ago. Exciting, isn't it? Like going back in time and standing there beside the painter, sensing the damp warmth of that deep, quiet place. There isn't a static square inch . . . it's all alive, growing! Yet what a marvelous silence! I dare say if this spot is still there, it's not far from the hell of a freeway, littered with tourist offal . . . picnic filth . . . Paintings like these shouldn't be hidden away. They're records of the wonderful

66

country America used to be. They should be hung where our children can see what we've sacrificed!"

Scott glanced quickly at Edward, conscious of having brushed against a throbbing wound.

"I didn't mean to hurt you," he said. "I think you know how sorry I am . . ."

"I don't expect people to tiptoe around me," Edward said.

"Thanks . . . I have a son . . . he's eighteen now. Perhaps because of him I care what happens to the generations next in line. I hope to God *you* won't stop working for them!"

Scott took the Gifford from Edward and placed both paintings carefully on the table. "Could I have some newspapers? And some string? We'd better be getting along. It's quite a drive. Sure you want to come?"

"Sure."

Scott put his hand on Edward's shoulder. "You rate a few days off. Your enemies will try to make something of it, of course. But your friends will wait for you to come back refreshed and strengthened, prepared to do battle again. You can't fail because you believe in yourself."

A stray thought trailing a tattered banner crossed Edward's consciousness: Ricardo's advice to believe not in himself but in God. Was that no more than a shift of responsibility? He made himself smile at Scott whose long painter's fingers tightened and then let go.

"You're going to be all right, Edward," he said.

Going to be? A second thought followed the first. And again there was the flutter of a torn flag.

"I hope so," he said again, but sharply this time. "Mrs. Littlefield will wrap the pictures for you. And while she's doing it, I suggest a glass of apple cider and some sugar cookies . . ."

"Cheers," Scott said. He gathered up his treasures and holding them against himself, against his heart, he followed

Edward to the kitchen. Murphy, who had heard the word "cookies" was there first.

They headed east for fifty miles, then north. Scott avoided the highways, taking alternate roads, old roads now neglected, the narrow pavements pitted, in places split by the frosts. It was hard to believe that a few years ago these had been well-traveled ways. They had linked town to town, farm to farm. Most of the blighting signboards had been abandoned; those that were still readable advertised motels and "eateries" on the Coast. During the hot summer months cattle stood in their shade, cud-chewing and tail-whisking, infinitely patient.

Scott drove well, but he was in no hurry. Now and then he stopped the rattling station wagon, and cutting off the engine, gazed at something in the landscape that attracted him: a stark gray farmhouse or a bare field or a distant stand of trees or an old drunk of a fence staggering around the curve of a hill.

Once when Edward let Murphy out near an apparently deserted barn, a dirty white hound came to investigate. The two big dogs touched noses, then bristling and mincing, their stiff tails vibrating, circled each other on tiptoe. But Murphy jumped back into the car when Edward whistled. The white hound looked forlornly after them as they drove away. Edward wondered whether he ought to take him along. Probably not. He must belong to somebody; there was fat on his bones.

Scott's studio stood on the brink of a cliff above the churning and foaming of the restless sea. Never, day or night, was there any pause in the attack of the breakers . . . they moved in from the horizon, built up, gathered strength, surged forward and broke with a thunderous crash against the cliffs. Then you could hear the hiss of that released force pushing between the rocks, draining off with a sucking sound only to be met by the next wave, and in its turn submerged.

The air in this place was laced with the iodine smell of kelp and on warm days the tangy sweetness of dwarf juniper.

The studio itself was built of field stones hauled down from the upland pastures and fitted together with great care so that the walls withstood the constant bombardment from below. A large window faced north; there were no others. This window was balanced at the opposite end of the building by a strong, squat chimney. The entrance on the sheltered side had the look of a fortress; a thick, panelled door had been removed from some old church and placed here to keep intruders at bay.

Inside it was cold and damp. Scott went ahead, finding his way about unerringly, and lighted a kerosene lamp. The sudden flare of the match and then the circle of yellow and blue flame blotted out the immense window and the last of the northern dusk.

"Come in," Scott called to Edward who had hesitated on the threshold. "I'll have a fire in a minute."

He shed his coat and set to work, emptying a basketfull of kindling on the hearth, then stacking logs wigwam fashion on a crackling explosion of sparks. Light played on the whitewashed walls and the beamed ceiling, and all at once the place was alive with color . . . Paintings. Paintings filling every available space. Stacks of them. Tables loaded with them. Chests filled with them. Edward wondered where Scott would find room for the Gifford and the Shurtleff. And as if he read his guest's mind, Scott said: "I'll hang them at Lucky River, not here. These are all my own. I avoid the intrusion of other men's concepts as much as possible." He seemed exhilarated, even excited by being in the presence of his

69

work. "I suppose you wonder how I can stand the sound of the sea? I suppose it's for the same reason that people leave their radios going full blast day and night. A sort of distraction."

"I like it, myself," Edward said. "The sea, I mean."

Scott tossed a heavy log on top of the others; it fell with a crash and, dusting off his hands, he turned to Edward.

"Are you as hungry as I am? There's some canned stuff here and I'll fix supper. But we'll sleep at the house. It's a mile from here, back from the sea in a meadow. Make yourself comfortable. What will Murphy want?"

Edward said: "Anything we ourselves have." He began to prowl along the walls, looking at Scott's work. There were perhaps a dozen portraits, sketches really, since most of them were unfinished. But landscapes predominated. Edward knew that these things would bring fabulous prices if and when they were sold. "Modernism" hadn't influenced this man at all. He painted what he saw; the result wasn't realistic in the photographic sense . . . recognizable, yes, but seen through the artist's sensibilities, touched by his imagination, his work evoked the viewer's own creative capacity, so that, looking, one shared the artist's vision.

He was busy, now, in a small galley where he lighted a two-burner stove "powered" by canned fuel. His eyes, hazel and shortsighted, were exaggerated by the thick lenses of horn-rimmed spectacles. He moved so that every gesture counted . . . no confusions here. He was as skillful at opening a can of baked beans as he was in outlining the structure of a human head; he gave you a feeling of being one with everything he could see or touch.

"Can I help?" Edward asked.

"No, thanks. Unless you'll clear off that table. Put the whole mess on the floor. And draw up a couple of chairs . . . Coffee?"

70

"I'm an addict," Edward admitted.

"But you don't smoke?"

"I never have."

"I remember. At school. I tried to introduce you to cigarettes made of corn-silk and toilet paper. You were game, but you vomited . . . Happy days!"

"Were they? You were lucky; you were expelled. You got out of it."

"Do you know why? I lacked mathematics. I made it, somehow, through grammar school, but when I got to Groton, I was done for. I have a blind spot. I can't balance a checkbook or add up a laundry list. That's why I didn't fly. I envied you up there, fighting clean. Down where I was, it was all muck and blood. You don't need to understand the differential calculus to stick a man with a bayonet. Thank God, I didn't have to. I was a fair shot but I never saw what I hit. It was more comfortable. If that's the word . . ."

"It will serve," Edward said. And there passed across his mind a picture . . . in full color . . . of Munich dissolving into orange dust.

"How did all this come about?" he asked, and made a sweeping gesture. "How does a man start to be a painter? How does he decide? You're the best, in my book, but when did you *know*?"

"Nothing else interests me, or ever has." Scott was frying something in a skillet and he had to shout above the pop of hot oil: "I suppose it's a desire to hang on to places or faces that excite me . . . not to lose them. That's why I hate to sell my stuff. And that's why it brings such prices. Once you're reluctant to part with your product the word gets out that it must be worth having and the dealers claw their way to your door offering anything, but anything!"

Edward laughed. It was the first time since the accident

71

that he had felt so much at ease. The room, the sound of the sea, the firelight, the company of an old friend added up to an unfamiliar harmony, a sense of safety . . . the library lamp again? When Scott asked him to find some plates and cups and to set the table, he went about the simple chore whistling softly. And when he sat down to the good meal his host had somehow conjured up, he dug in with appetite. Murphy, too, slurped and smacked under the table. It was possible to listen to Scott's monologue without at the same time struggling to control the Absolute Evil at the pit of his own mind. He seemed to be floating free, detached from suffering, buoyed up on the lightest possible element. And for a moment he knew again what it was to relax.

Scott was saying: "I'm always glad when Spring comes. I could spend the winter here but Mitzi couldn't stand it. Lucky River suits both of us . . . we like people but in small doses. For weeks at a time we're quite alone and enjoy it. I don't know what I'd do if I had to live with a gregarious woman. Mitzi is busy at home from morning to night. She never resents my being shut away in my workroom or wandering around the frozen countryside by myself. You've met her, haven't you?"

"Once. At your show in New York."

"We put in an appearance because it was good business. It went to prove that I'm not the creation of a dealer and a press agent! We were dressed in our best and very amiable and approachable. Mitzi was a hit with both the buyers and the lookers."

Scott grinned.

"We took in over fifty thousand dollars! But do you know, Edward, I wanted to buy back the whole lot!"

He got up and went to the galley for coffee. And suddenly, unreasonably, Edward felt once more that sharp stab of dread. If only there were some way to keep Scott from

72

saying what he was about to say! Some way to head him off! Three years ago he had painted Valerie's portrait. She didn't like it and Scott had refused to let Edward see it. There was danger, now, that the artist might mention it, apologize or explain or even offer the portrait to Edward to "comfort" him in his loss . . . Until Scott sat down and began once more to praise his own wife, Edward's stomach was tied into knots, the food stuck in his throat and the damnable throbbing began behind his eyes.

It was a close call but mercifully it passed.

When he could concentrate again, Scott was saying that he regretted his own lack of interest in politics.

"Frankly, I don't know what Government's all about. I don't *want to know! I'm perfectly willing to let you fellows* handle the affairs of state. And yet I'm a sentimentalist about this country. The original idea, which you seem to be reviving . . . the moral integrity and sense of personal responsibility . . . I'm for it, Edward. More power to you. I daresay I'm a romantic. I believe in the American image: would you call it great-heartedness? The heroic ideal? I saw it not once but over and over again during the war. If it's ever shattered by skepticism we're sunk. But sunk."

"Well then?" Edward asked.

"The country isn't going to hell," Scott said, "because *I* don't vote."

He pushed his plate aside and with the tines of a fork drew a circle on the table top.

"So. I don't vote. I don't because I'm not intelligent enough about national affairs to have convictions about the qualifications of any one man. But there *is* something I *can* do. See here . . . Let's say this circle is America. A sort of pond. And here . . ." he made a dot on the edge of the circle . . . "am I. I pick up a pebble and toss it into the water. Here.

73

It starts a ring of ripples, like this, and that ring expands and expands as it moves across the surface. A pebble splashes here and is felt all the way around the pond. So. No gesture, no thought, no deed, no kindness, no sin is lost. We must take care to start the right circles because so help me God they'll reach the farthest shore, bearing our signature!"

Scott broke off with an embarrassed grin: "Imagine my talking to *you* like this!"

"Why not to me?"

"I'm not even certain whether you're a Republican or a Democrat! Or how the Senate and the House function. Or the processes of election. That's a fact! I haven't time to understand these things, and I'm a miser about time. The pebble I throw into the pond is beauty . . . that's my heritage and my contribution. I'm a good painter. The eyes I see with are American, just as the heart that beats in me is American. What I'm saying is: 'Hang on to this, you poor bastards, while you still can'!"

He removed the thick-lensed spectacles. His eyes were gentle, and somehow myopia made him seem vulnerable. He could be hurt, Edward thought, but less often than most men and not so deeply since he was protected by his indifference to criticism. No use arguing with him, then. Hear him out. Besides, there could be no harm in a man as talented as this. He seemed to believe . . . and he went on at some length to say so . . . that he was serving American far more effectively than by taking part in the insensate mob violence that was breaking through the crust of the country like a crop of poisonous mushrooms. Far better to paint that sea out there and those wet cliffs or a farmer or a fisherman than to bqp a rioter with a broken bottle or to kick a corrupt inciter in the rump.

"I do know some of the steps you've taken," he said, putting the spectacles on again, "to cut through prejudice to the truth. Perhaps if you live and can keep ahead of the mounting national frustration, we might see your Plan realized. We might have a goal, a purpose once more . . . and no more sops thrown to the masses who sit in stadiums gorged on pop and hot dogs, each with a transistor radio stuck to one of his ears! If it's not baseball, it's sex . . . the transistor radio going along as usual, even into bed!"

Edward laughed, "All of this has happened before," he said.

"Rome?"

"If there *was* an Atlantis it probably happened there. We've settled for a scientific revolution, right enough, but who knows, in Tut's day they might have known everything we know and then some!"

Edward paused, thinking of what Ricardo had said: "We advance step by step." The teaching of Someone who lived two thousand years ago perhaps didn't apply to conditions here and now. Man was beginning to realize that he wouldn't be punished for his sins, and so, excused from a tussle with his conscience, he experimented with lust and violence and dishonesty. No one seemed to notice or to care. But when he finally arrived at a whole new concept of morality, the old teachings would come around again. They would, because they were valid.

"We can't change things too fast, Scott," he said aloud. "When you try to, you come up against a mass rebellion. People want what they've always had even though it isn't enough any more. They turn against anyone who asks for a few centuries of work and sacrifice. It's easier to use the bomb and kill each other off down to the last poor ape in the jungles."

"Why do you keep on then?" Scott demanded.

Edward thought for a moment. Then he shook his head.

"You *want* to be President?"

"Do you want to paint masterpieces?"

"It's not the same thing," Scott retorted with a flash of temper. "A painter is responsible to no one but himself. A President can't be himself without permission."

Edward said nothing. In the sudden silence the sea made itself heard. And he thought how old it was, how indifferent, how cruel and how beautiful . . . for him and for millions to follow him, a mystery . . .

While Scott washed the dishes . . . he was, he confessed, a rabid cleaner-upper . . . Edward got his permission to look through the water-colors and drawings stacked on shelves and leaning against the walls. There were many sketches of Mitzi and at least a dozen tries to capture a round-eyed child wearing a wet slicker in the gray light of a rainy day. The yellow of the slicker and its reflection on the child's chin must have caused him trouble. When he noticed Edward's interest he called out from the galley that he intended to tackle the problem "life-size," and could only hope that the child hadn't grown over the winter; if he waited much longer she'd grow right out of his vision of her. The yellow light was in her eyes, and in some of the rain drops quivering on the oily surface of the slicker . . . "Yet the whole effect is grayed by the drenching sky . . . over all, a sort of premonition: buttercup dust and storm . . . Do you know what I'm trying to say?"

"I think so," Edward said. He put the sketch back and went to the next stack. These were mostly portraits, meticulously drawn, and Edward suspected that Scott hadn't been at his best when he did them. Either he didn't really like people who came to him to be immortalized, or else the task bored him. These were arrogant faces, challenging the artist to earn his fee: "Be sure to make me look as beautiful or as important as I'm not!"

76

But at the bottom of the stack there was one that even upside down struck a note purely its own. Edward turned it rightside up and there, with a white flash of a smile, was Megan Donahue.

"Who's this?"

Scott, wiping a dish, looked over. "Oh," he said. "That's Megan. Don't you know her?"

Edward didn't say. He carried the sketch closer to the lamp and for a long time studied the likeness that seemed as alive as the girl herself. Above an indication of the fuzzy red sweater, her face was rosy, her eyes smudged-in as Edward remembered them. But it was the merry look of her that made the portrait so startling . . . she seemed to be enjoying herself, to be happy for no particular reason, simply happy.

"You mean," Scott demanded, "that you've never met Megan Donahue? That makes you unique, Edward! She knows everyone on earth. And calls them by their first names . . . right down the list from kings and queens to fighters and senators and jockeys and who else . . ."

"I've met her," Edward interrupted, "but she didn't call me Edward."

"She will. You're a bit formidable, you know. Even Megan would hesitate to chuck you under that jutting chin of yours."

Scott stood beside Edward; he, too, studied the portrait. "She sat for me last summer . . . just as you see her, with the wind in her hair and love in her eyes . . ."

"For you?"

"She loves the whole human race. She's the lovingest woman on earth." Scott's eyes flashed behind his spectacles. "Promiscuous? Who's to say? I've never slept with her, myself, although I've wanted to: Mitzi was jealous and she made it impossible. Megan isn't the sort of woman you can enjoy in some hide-out, sneaking an hour when no one's looking. You need an eternity, and an eternity wouldn't be enough. Do I make myself clear?"

"Perfectly," Edward said. "I take it you were in love with her . . . still are, perhaps."

Scott shook his head. "If I am, it's not with Megan . . . it's with what she made me feel about me, myself! She does it to every man she meets. God knows it may be a trick, but I don't think so. When you're with her you're the man you've always wanted to be. She makes you feel exceptional . . . better looking and stronger than you are, more talented than you are. She has ways of evoking the youth you've put aside. Suddenly you want to kick your heels like a spring lamb and frolic through the grass."

Scott took off his spectacles as if in dimming his own vision he also made himself less visible.

"Mitzi knows this. For years, she's watched Megan at her sad, wonderful game of make-believe. She's always turning up at our house with some bemused celebrity in tow. Famous singers. Conductors. Writers. Scientists. Generals . . . You can't keep her out. She has ways with barricades. She'll walk into a tycoon's stronghold and in ten minutes has him serving champagne at poolside. It's *gala* wherever she happens to be. Old men turn into boys and boys long to be men. Not that she's a beauty . . ."

Scott gestured toward the picture.

"Other women spend fortunes on hairdressers. Megan's hair . . . well! She has good legs, of course . . ."

"You've noticed," Edward broke in.

"Didn't you?"

Edward let this pass. It seemed best to remark simply that she had seemed to him to be an extraordinarily disheveled female.

"She can be as elegant as the Duchess of Windsor," Scott protested. "She knows how to dress, only it's not the most

78

important thing in her life. Besides, she can't afford clothes."

"That's surprising."

"You mean men? Not on your life. She pays her own way. She had a husband once who was worth a lot, but when she left him she refused to accept alimony. She's been walking a financial tight-rope ever since."

"She's a reporter, isn't she?"

Scott grinned. "She can't write a coherent sentence," he said. "Have you ever received one of her letters?"

"No."

"They look like sand-piper tracks! All uphill and around the back of the paper. Dots and dashes and exclamation points. They offend my sense of order but I'm always glad when I find one in the post box."

Scott resumed his thick lensed disguise.

"Don't misunderstand me," he said. "Mitzi is the one I want. That's the way it is with men who fall in love with Megan. They don't marry her. For a few weeks they play her game . . . and then suddenly they're gone . . . back to their wives and their careers, invigorated, rejuvenated, full of fight."

"And grateful?" Edward asked.

"I doubt it. They've sent her flowers . . . never jewels . . . and that seems to satisfy their sense of obligation. 'Great fun,' they say of her. And the next time they meet her, they tell her how successful they are, how rich, how much in demand . . . and introduce her to their wives, who snub her. Not *Mitzi*! Don't jump to conclusions!"

"I didn't say anything."

"You were thinking!"

Both men laughed. And for a moment in companionable silence they stared at the portrait. Edward recalled what Eithne had said: "She's a tramp. A dime a dozen in Washington." Strange, how women know instinctively when

79

they are confronted by a threat to their security in love and find themselves helpless to combat the most powerful enemy of all: sex more potent than their own. He wanted suddenly to know all there was to know about Megan Donahue.

Scott said: "She's a lady, whatever that means. Her people are 'gentry' in Ireland. She could go back there and settle into the musty, misty hard-riding life, but she won't accept a dole from her family. You, of all men, should understand why she feels like this. It's not easy, but she gets along as well as the hordes you've released from welfare grants, learning the hard way what freedom is, but learning."

Scott closed the galley door and went back to the fireplace, kicking a renewed spark of life into the half-charred log. Then turning his back to the warmth he went on: "I've said very little to explain the real Megan, to make her clear to you. In a poem somewhere it says 'nothing is lost that gives itself to love.' She's given much and has lost nothing . . . sometimes she makes me think of a little moon touching with illusion everything she meets in her drifting. And sometimes she's a child's balloon jerking and tugging at the string that holds her back from the sky. Women like Megan are rare in these days of diamond-hard women who glitter but don't shine . . . Mitzi shines, too, but in another way . . . She's jealous of Megan and suffers because she thinks I hanker . . ."

"Don't you?"

After a pause, Scott admitted that he probably did. For that reason he had just decided to burn Megan's portrait . . . for Mitzi's sake. And for his own. Because even if it were hidden away, he'd know it was there and could look at it when he was alone; her face always got through to him like a thrill of longing. He went back to the table and picked up the square of beaver-board. "Here goes," he said with a sudden tightening of his lips, and turned to the fire.

"No," Edward said. He reached out and grabbed Scott's

80

arm. "Let me have it! Let me keep it until you're too old to fear what it does to you. Then it can hang in a museum and do honor to your name."

Scott's fingers let go.

"I daresay you're right. Take it. And I'll tell Mitzi . . . No. I won't need to tell her! She knows. She knew the instant Megan moved out of my heart."

Scott put the portrait on the table, saying that he'd wrap it properly in the morning. And then he said a momentous thing, not knowing that he did: "I was glad when Valerie changed her mind about *her* portrait."

"Changed her mind? I didn't know she had!"

"Then it *was* a secret," Scott said with a startled, questioning look. "Yes. She drove to Lucky River from Charleston about two weeks before the accident, and paid for the portrait and took it away with her. She said she was giving it to someone she loved very much . . . you, of course."

"But she never did give it to me."

"She meant to; I'm sure of that."

"I don't understand," Edward began. At first, surprise held the deeper reaction in check. "I talked to her every day from Washington. She never told me she'd seen you. I had no idea . . ."

"For your birthday, perhaps," Scott interrupted.

"My birthday's in January. Someone she loved very much? She said that?"

"It's not likely I'd forget what she said. She was emotionally upset. She must indeed have loved you very much. More than I believed she *could* love."

Scott broke off.

"Forgive me, Edward, but when she sat for me, I had a chance to study her . . . not only her beauty . . . that was

81

evident . . . but the woman herself. I felt she was incapable of feeling anything deeply."

Edward turned away to conceal his anguish. Always alert, Murphy came out from under the table.

"But when she appeared at Lucky River that day," Scott went on, "I saw a different woman. She was feeling, all right . . . as if pierced through every layer of consciousness to the inmost heart . . . She couldn't have plucked that arrow out if she had wanted to: the pain of it was too sweet. *You, Edward. You, of course!* Perhaps I shouldn't have told you this. But isn't it better than not knowing? Somehow I've always felt that you weren't sure of her. You were the suppliant, she the remote goddess withholding mercy. Am I right? I am! You don't need to tell me . . ."

"My birthday's in January," Edward repeated, his voice curiously deadened and flat.

"To hell with that, then," Scott broke in. "She asked me not to tell you. It was to be a surprise, she said. That's all I know. Perhaps it was her way of cracking through her reticences . . . her damn good manners! Possibly she was a savage inside, a lover to tear a man apart. And couldn't . . . didn't dare . . . show it. Some women are like that all their pitiful lives. They die without having given. If I were you, Edward, I think I'd be glad she was spared the rest of it. Grateful for that much, at least."

Suddenly he leaned over the lamp and blew on the flame. The room was dark then save for the cats' eyes on the hearth.

"Time to turn in," he said. And Edward followed him out into a cold, starry night and along a path that climbed between low stone walls to a house in a field. The sound of the sea receded and then was lost. Neither man spoke until Scott had opened a door, and striking a match, had lighted a row of candles in pewter sticks that stood on a chest in a whitewashed hallway.

82

"I'll show you where you'll sleep," he said, "and then I'll bring you some blankets and pillows. There'll be frost tonight . . ."

When he had glanced into the low-ceilinged bedroom, Edward said: "I'd like to take Murphy for a run. If I don't turn him out now, he'll be restless all night."

"I'll leave the door open," Scott said. "If you want to speak to me for any reason, shout, because I sleep like a granite slab. My room's down the hall . . . Good night."

Edward thanked him and with a gesture invited the big dog to follow him out into the starry dark again.

Never such stars. The whole arch of sky was filled with shaking, glittering crystal spheres and five-pointed planets. So bright that it was easy to follow the path back to the cliffs and then along their crest. The way here was narrow and uneven; spikey juniper branches caught at Edward's socks; he felt scratches around his ankles, across his insteps, but ignored them. Risking a sudden stumble, he didn't look down, but up at the sky. Never such stars. Never so many. The sweep of the Milky Way was like a powdering of crushed crystals. And there were many falling stars that ignited for an instant then plunged, thin threads of fire that diminished and were quenched somewhere out there . . .

Edward waited for the dreaded physical symptoms to reappear. When they didn't, he climbed down to the surface of a flat rock that jutted like a platform over the water. He sat down, his arms around his knees. The sea was quiet, now; it moved toward the land in long swells that seemed to feel along the cliffs, lifting against the barrier, exploring silently, then falling as silently back into the depths. Here and there the starlight struck a flash of silver. Edward thought that this was the first time he had been as alone as this in many years. Here there were no pushing, gaping crowds, no cameras focused on him, no security guards, no mikes held to his lips.

He might have been the most obscure man among millions of obscure men, not one of a few hundred who had lifted themselves out of the anonymous into the conspicuous. He felt as if all the props had been removed from his ego, leaving him weak and helpless. What was he doing here, sitting in the midnight dark alone? Was he as ill as Eithne feared? "Take hold," he said to himself. "Take firm hold. Make certain. Now . . . Am I safe? Am I sane?"

And he made himself think of what Scott had told him: "She loved you." He made himself go back over his life with Valerie, seeing her, and himself, in the light of that possibility: "She loved you." All the way from his first seeing her through the flowers at that dinner table to the moment at Charleston when she got into the plane unwillingly, bending to his will. He forced himself to look at his memory of her . . . not the broken creature lying in the gully, but the living woman. *Had* she loved him? In all their ten years together, she hadn't said. Then he must have failed somehow to understand why. The lack must have been in himself, so that the two halves of their man-woman relationship couldn't, or wouldn't meet. The circle was never completed, the longing never consummated or satisfied. There was always that gap, that separation . . . And yet Scott had seemed so certain . . . If he was right, then Valerie had agreed to fly with him that day, not because she had something to gain by taking such a chance, but because she couldn't deny the man she loved anything . . . Didn't the whole thing hinge on the portrait? Was she perhaps waiting until he was in the White House? The portrait to hang there? Was that the secret? But suppose he weren't nominated, next year or five years from now? If it were the evanescent immortality of a place in the sad procession of First Ladies . . . it was too soon to count on that! Why, then, had she changed her mind? And where was the portrait now? Would Valerie's grandmother know?

4

In spite of his wool shirt and a sweater, Edward felt cold. He lay back against the rock, and Murphy, who had seemed afraid of the sheer drop into the sea, moved close. The warmth of the dog's body was welcome and Edward thought: "Thanks, Murphy."

Strange, that so far there had been no pain behind his eyes. It was only a step to the edge of the cliff but he felt no compelling urge to take that step and to let himself fall into the breathing, silver-flaked depth . . . The circles moving away from the splash! Like those circles Scott had drawn on the table top: no deed, no sin, no mistake, no cowardice, no cruelty, no weakness, no betrayal, no treachery to go unnoticed . . . no strength, no decency, no loyalty, no good, no service to go unnoticed. The circles advancing across the world, around the world, and beyond . . . signed and sealed!

And suddenly Edward was conscious of the shape and size of the globe. He put his hand down on the cold of the rock and thought: "This is part of my earth." He felt its roundness, its suspension in the midst of those myriad stars, the speed of its great heavy endless turning, the dark of it and the light of it. He thought of the people living on its surface, carried around and around in space, each limited to just so many years . . . a very short time in which to learn what must be learned. And no real certainty of anything beyond, any reward for effort! Just keep going as well and as long as you can. Ricardo's God wasn't a sure thing. Who said that if there weren't a God, man would invent one? But there was something holding it all together . . . if not Someone then Something. Since there's no way of knowing, why speculate? Either accept as true the existence of an afterlife or dodge the issue entirely and postpone the reckoning until the time comes when you must face up to it. This Valerie and the boys had done. Too soon!

"Because I tried to outfly a hurricane," Edward thought. "To impress them? To show off? I suppose so, God help me."

What was that? Had he asked for help? Had he expected absolution? Instinctively, he looked up, saw no Divine Face, heard no Divine Voice. Only the stars and a strange crackling as one of them plunged from the apex trailing a long tail of sparks.

Edward felt the muscles of his arms tightening; the whiplash struck at the back of his neck and pain filled his eyes, his skull. He was not safe, after all. This thing could overwhelm him at any moment, anywhere he happened to be . . .

He stumbled to his feet. Murphy jumped up and aside and when Edward urged him out of the way: "Go back!" began to whine and shiver. It must be now, Edward thought. This time nothing must interfere. It would look as if he had gone too close to the edge, had leaned too far over and had fallen. The man floating down there, carried along the cliffs by the black, slow swells, would never again have to realize that he had killed a woman he loved and who may have loved him. A man who had striven to help his countrymen and had sacrificed his wife and sons! He kicked Murphy out of his way.

Scott had followed him.

"Edward!" he shouted from the path and slid down, digging his heels in, starting an avalanche of dirt and stones.

"Get away from there, you damned fool!" Grabbing Edward's arm, he jerked him back from the rim, almost threw him to his knees. "What in hell do you think you're doing?"

Edward didn't say, but Murphy began to bark and caper and show his teeth in a wolf's grin.

"You sure scared me," Scott said unsteadily.

"I'm sorry."

"You were gone for more than an hour. I was anxious because I know how dangerous these cliffs are. If you don't mind, I'll stay with you. It might be safer."

He indicated that Edward was to take the lead and they both scrambled up to the path.

"It's late," Scott said with a note of apology. "I suggest that we try to get some sleep."

"By all means. And thanks. I *was* close! I think it must have been the water down there that attracted me. It was full of silver . . ."

"Phosphorus," Scott said.

"No. Starlight."

Murphy stayed close to Edward. He must have resented the kick because he whined . . . a thin whine, like a whistle. Edward felt the dog's cold nose against his hand.

"I'll explain later," he said aloud.

"How's that?"

"Nothing."

There was embarrassment between them, a shamefaced reluctance to discuss what had happened.

In the house they said good night again.

Edward invited Murphy to lie beside him, and in a cautious whisper told him: "I was afraid you might jump in after me. Well. It didn't happen. Forgive me, old man." For this, he was licked, and he supposed, forgiven. Presently Murphy curled upon himself and slept, but Edward lay awake for many hours. He felt as he always did after these "compulsions", both exhausted and clear-minded. By the time Scott woke and began to move about the unfamiliar house, Edward had decided to resign from office. He was no longer fit to take responsibility. He would stop off at Easterly long enough to settle with the Littlefields. Then he would drive to Washington, advise the President of his decision and write off the effort of the years. After that . . .

It didn't occur to him that his cry for help had been heard. Scott was no divine lifeguard! Just a friend who had happened along in time . . .

Scott spent the morning with two carpenters from the nearest town, who helped him to remove the heavy wooden blinds on the west side of the house and to uncover the pipes and the pump. They were young fellows, their strong forearms tattooed with serpents and flags. If they recognized Edward, they had no interest in him. At twelve o'clock sharp they stopped work and sat on the back steps to eat their lunch. Murphy was too polite to beg; he kept his distance, licking his jowls, and caught bits of bread and meat with a snap of his white teeth.

"Smart dog you've got there," one of the men said. "Ever

hunt with him?"

"No," Edward said.

"Too bad. He'd take training. Want to sell him?"

"No."

"I'll give you fifty dollars.."

Edward thought: "I bought him for a hundred." And recalled folding Megan Donahue's small fingers over the money. Aloud he said: "He doesn't really belong to me. You might say he's collateral."

The men gave him a slow, appraising look. They would have smiled only they seemed to be congenitally unable to express amusement. And suddenly feeling discomfited, as if hit in the face by a rotten egg, Edward whistled to Murphy and went into the house.

Before he drove away from the place Scott stood for a moment looking at it as if trying to fix the image, every detail of it, in his consciousness. Edward sensed that things meant more to Scott than people ever could. He could grieve over a fallen tree, feel compassion for a deserted house, admiration for the heroic struggle of a plant to survive the freezing winters of this bleak land. "I'm always happiest here," he said, climbing into the station wagon and starting off with a jerk. "I'm glad I won't live to see it overrun with robots."

"How do you mean?"

"I won't be alive," Scott said, "to witness the final degradation. Thank God for that."

He didn't explain what he meant and Edward didn't ask. Something had happened to dull their companionship; probably the incident on the cliff . . . Scott may have guessed the truth of it, and blamed himself for discussing Valerie. He seemed anxious to get Edward back to Easterly and, avoiding the old roads he headed for the freeways and drove too fast for comfort. There were no stops for coffee and hamburgers. Once a motorcycle cop waved them over and had already made note of the license number and was about to get Scott's name when he became aware of Edward. The familiar look of recognition and surprise sharpened in his eyes and he touched his helmet with the tips of his gloved fingers.

"Okay, sir. Get going. But watch it."

The Easterly gate was open. A county patrol car was parked outside; as Scott drove in, it moved off toward the village.

"They must have wondered where you'd gone," Scott said. "I should have telephoned . . ."

"I'm glad you didn't," Edward said.

Another car waited in front of the house and Edward saw that it belonged to Valerie's grandmother . . . it was the limousine that had brought Valerie and the boys to the Charleston airfield. The driver . . . an elderly man wearing the conventional whipcord uniform of a family chauffeur . . . was dozing at the wheel. Twilight was deepening but the house was still unlighted. And as Scott parked, Mrs. Littlefield hurried out from the kitchen wing.

"I thought you'd never come," she said. "It's been a terrible day! I didn't know where you'd gone. I couldn't tell them. They've been questioning me for hours . . ."

"I'm sorry," Edward said. He turned to Scott. "Will you come in?"

"Thank you, no," Scott said. He seemed to relax suddenly, as if he had discharged his responsibility. "I must go along. Mitzi's waiting for me." He handed the portrait of Megan to Edward. "If you still want it . . .?"

"I do. Of course."

There was a brief pause. Then Scott said: "Take care of yourself, Edward. And come to us when you can. We'd be honored . . ."

90

"Oh, go to hell," Edward said with a quick laugh.

They shook hands, forgiveness and understanding in the brief, hard contact. Murphy jumped out and ran to the kitchen door.

"Now," Edward said, as the station wagon rattled down the drive, "let's have it, Mrs. Littlefield."

"*Have* it?" she repeated with a touch of scorn. "*Have* it? They made me feel like a spy! The telephone's been ringing all day. I haven't had time to listen to the radio, but Mr. Littlefield tells me those news fellows never let up. You'd have thought . . ."

"I see my wife's grandmother's here," Edward interrupted, glancing at the parked limousine.

"She came at four o'clock. I didn't know when to expect you, but she decided to wait. I gave her tea in the library. The others left when I remembered your friend's name. Scott. Was I right?"

"You were right. Yes."

"They ran in a pack to the telephone, and then they drove away . . ."

"*Who* left? Who *were* these people?"

"Police, I suppose. The F.B.I.? They were upstairs and down, all over the barn and through the woods and along the beach . . . looking, looking, under bushes and even into the boat sheds!"

"Don't worry, Mrs. Littlefield," Edward said with a smile. "It's all over. I'll answer the phone from now on. And tomorrow I'll be gone."

"I must say I'm glad," the caretaker's wife said with a cold smile.

Valerie's grandmother was sitting in the chair Ricardo had occupied, neatly composed, her small, delicately shod feet together, her back straight, her white-gloved hands holding a sable scarf. Around her throat, irridescent against the dull black of her dress, a double strand of small pearls.

She looked up at Edward with what might have been a flash of fear in her eyes. Or perhaps it was panic, as if she had ventured too close to an unsolicited confession and realized suddenly how far she'd fall if she stumbled.

"I'm glad you're here, Edward," she said, and gave him a tightly gloved hand; he bent down and kissed her cheek. "I wasn't really worried," she said, "but this *has* been an upsetting experience!"

"I'm sorry."

"Secret Service men swarming all over the house and beating the thickets . . ."

"I hope they didn't question you!"

"But they did! Why did you disappear without telling anyone where you'd be? Have you forgotten that your safety is a matter of great concern to the country? Or don't you care?"

"I'd care," Edward said flatly, "if I thought it was so."

He put Megan Donahue's portrait on the table and lighted the lamp. "I can't understand all the excitement," he said. "I came here for a few days of peace. Nothing sinister. I daresay the place has been watched ever since I arrived."

He sat down, facing her, leaning forward, his hands clasped. He felt suddenly old and exhausted.

"It was good of you to come," he managed to say, "but I don't know why you did. Couldn't you have phoned and spared yourself the trip? I could have told you: I'm all right."

"You sound like a television comedian," she said with a smile, expecting him to get the implication. When he didn't, she frowned. "I hope you don't intend to resign?"

He didn't answer at once. He decided that she was being both loyal and kind. He had always respected her because she

92

refused to lower her standard. Her sense of honor was more masculine than feminine; she asked no quarter, accepted no favors; if there was any defect in her character, it was vanity, a deep-rooted conviction that whatever she did was right . . . but this, Edward knew, stemmed from pride of class, the aristocrat's defense against the intrusion of the less privileged. Her sort was due to disappear, and soon, from the American scene. In the meantime she would remain faithful to her concept of correct behaviour and would go to her grave indifferent to the New Order.

"I've driven over a thousand miles," she said now, "to talk to you. Perhaps to help you let go of your grief. Oh, Edward, I do feel deeply sorry for you! You loved your wife and sons and you've lost all of them."

"But must we discuss it here and now?"

"You would have lost them anyway," she said cautiously, as if feeling for a safe step forward.

"In due time, of course," Edward said. "However, I might have been fortunate enough to go first!"

But he was too late to head her off. Her hands shook and beneath a delicate brushing of powdered rouge she looked her age. Then she braced herself and said, "Valerie was going to leave you, Edward."

"That's impossible."

"You think so? She was going to leave you and take your sons with her."

"I don't believe it."

"You know how strong and determined she was. How ambitious. She married you because she believed that some day you'd be President."

"Nonsense. There was no certainty of that! There isn't now."

"Perhaps. But she was tired of waiting. She decided that it would be a long time before the people listened to you or

93

followed you. If indeed they ever did."

Edward sat without moving, still bent forward, his hands clasped. He tried to realize the meaning of what he had heard. At first he thought he'd refuse to let her go on; a decisive word from him would put an end to the conversation. But then he realized that to drop the matter here would leave him listening for the other shoe. He said, "I was under the impression that Valerie loved me."

"She never loved you, Edward. This is hard for me to say. But it might help you to know . . ."

"Know what?"

"That she loved someone else."

"If she did," Edward said, keeping the anger out of his voice, "she would have told me."

"She meant to."

He got up and stood on the hearth, flushed and shaken. "You knew about this?"

"I guessed it."

"You *guessed* it!"

"For a long time, yes . . . I guessed it. There were certain things I couldn't understand . . . her many trips to Europe, without you, for instance. Her restlessness and melancholy and then, a year ago, a sudden brilliance . . . as if she had opened a secret door and stood on the threshold bathed in light . . . Surely, you noticed?"

Edward shook his head. It was true; he hadn't noticed. Valerie had always looked "brilliant." But what of a "secret" door?

"Are you sure," he asked, "that you don't imagine all of this? There *is* another man . . . You're sure?"

"She met him two years ago, in Rome," the grandmother said. "A bold, fascinating Milanese. An industrialist. But titled."

"Ah," Edward interrupted with an involuntary snort of

94

contempt. "Titled, too! *Well!*"

"Never mind his name," she said. "I don't think you should know it."

"I don't want to."

"All you need to know," she said, "is that Valerie wanted him. Not you. She wanted his way of life. Not yours. Oh, Edward, if you had played the game of politics, had bought your way up, as you could have . . . Valerie would have followed you to the top! She came to me when she was twelve years old and I watched her grooming herself for high estate, but not preparing herself to *deserve* it! She told me that she had decided to divorce you because you had gone as far as you'll ever go. She said you were an idealist, not a fighting realist, and that she had no intention of sharing your decline. That after the election, you'd be set aside and forgotten."

"She must have hated me," Edward thought, but he said nothing.

"She was ambitious," the grandmother went on, not watching him now, as if she knew she'd get no help from him. "She was a woman who had to win, to be admired and envied. She couldn't face a future here in this house with you. No further excitement. No risks . . . Only a trickle of old friends . . . old men, most of them . . . rehashing their part in shaping the New Society . . ."

"There are worse destinies," Edward interrupted, still pushing back the anger that was rising in him like a black, sticky tide.

"Not for a woman like Valerie," the grandmother said. "Can't you see why? Life only half over for her ... . and you, her husband, dedicated, humane, another gentle rail-splitter. Or that other? The cruel, dark splendor of a reckless Latin!"

She shook her head. "Better let her go, Edward! Forget her, and for your sons' sakes, go back and win . . ."

"The portrait?" Edward interrupted. "What became of it?"

"You knew about that?"

"Scott told me. Yes."

"She sent it to Italy. To him. A letter came from him the day after the accident. Of course I opened it and read it. He thanked her for the portrait and said his villa was at her disposal . . . He expected her in a few weeks. Wait . . . I have it here . . ."

She groped in her hand bag for a folded sheet of paper and held it toward Edward. "Perhaps you'd better see for yourself." he noticed the word *carissima* but nothing else and shook his head. She put the letter back, closing the purse with a snap. "Very well. You're probably right. I'm glad no one knew about this. It might have given the authorities a reason to believe you wanted her to die and planned to die with her. It would have been said that you had reason . . ."

"Good God!" Edward shouted. "What a thought!"

"Nowadays, one is never surprised by criminal impulses in men of high position," she said sharply. And then, with a sudden note of compassion in her voice she said: "At least you didn't lose your sons to another man!"

"That couldn't have happened. I could have stoped her."

"I wonder. Hadn't she told you? She told me. She meant to fly to Italy at once, taking the boys with her. She wasn't coming back. And the next move would have been yours. Ruin for you, so soon before the election! Oh, Edward, if you give up now, for any reason, if you resign, she'll know it! Even in her grave she'll know it and gloat. Don't let her!"

Mrs. Littlefield was at the door. "Mr. Littlefield's come for me," she said. "In case you want supper, I left cold chicken in the ice-box."

Murphy had followed her. He looked questioningly at Edward, then crossed and flopped down with a gusty sigh.

"I fed the dog," Mrs. Littlefield said. "I'll come first thing in the morning. Will there be two for breakfast?"

Edward glanced at Valerie's grandmother, but she shook her head and stood, lifting the silky sable to her shoulders. He noticed the flowery fragrance Valerie had always used, had perhaps inherited, like the patrician cut of her features, from this woman.

"I'll drive as far as I can tonight," she said. "Tomorrow, I'll be with Eithne in New York." She went toward Edward, offering her cheek. "Good bye. Never mind coming out to the car."

But he followed her and stood in the driveway watching the limousine and Mr. Littlefield's pickup until they had disappeared.

At the last moment he said all the expected polite things. The small gloved hand waved behind the closed window and he saw her pale, troubled face, the clouded violet eyes. As the car rolled smoothly away, he thought with a stab of wry humor: *the Queen Mother* . . .

Now it was dark, the air icy and very still. There were no stars. It was very cold. Strange . . . in March! The brief spring was bracing itself for a retreat beneath the freezing soil. A promise ignored, set aside, perhaps for a month or longer. Winter was on its furious turnabout way again . . .

He couldn't face entering the house . . . not until he'd pulled himself together. He was shaking with anger. The written word *"Carissima"* lay across his mind like a burn . . . As there was still a trace of daylight, he decided to walk it off. Walk *what* off? Humiliation, he supposed. He could endure insult and physical hurt, but not betrayal. A stranger had stabbed him in the back. He didn't know his attacker's name, or how he looked, or where he lived. And Valerie had enjoyed this man . . . in what bed, in what house, in what city, where? The thought of that intimacy, secret and dishonest, sickened him. He felt a need to vomit.

He called Murphy and went around the house. Then, cutting across the lawn, which was already crusting with the cold, he plunged through the wood, straddled a low stone wall and took off along the upper road. Once many years ago this rough way had been in use between the main buildings and the cowsheds. Now it was overgrown with long blackberry vines, strong enough to trip the unwary. Edward could remember the warm sweet cattle odor and how, as a boy, he had watched the hired man at the milking, enjoying the metal ping of the jets in the tin pails.

Now it was quite dark; splinters of snow stung Edward's eyelids, and suddenly he was possessed by utter terror and loneliness, as if he were the only man left alive on a frozen planet. This was worse than jealousy and the fury of defeat in love. Murphy must have sensed the turmoil in his master's mind, and feared it; he whined, as he had that time on the cliff when he was kicked aside. But he stayed close.

The road grew very rough, full of clods and stones, and it was impossible not to stumble. Edward became aware of a new smell in the air: the pig enclosures must be near by . . . the years hadn't eliminated that odor. And he remembered when, as a boy, he had been permitted to feed the grunters; they were kept very clean . . . there were no filthy sties at Easterly . . . and yet that odor had persisted. Edward thought: "They were born fearing the butcher's knife." And then it had happened to them, and they knew what the suffering they dreaded was like. Their monument? Only this sour smell . . . this slop smell. The fear smell . . . Here in the dark, where no one ever passes, or cares . . .

98

Beyond the cow-barn the road frayed out. Edward turned back. He could no longer see the house . . . it was hidden by the falling snow; but he found his way to the garage and swung open the doors, revealing an even darker dark, and a silvery glinting where the great Rolls stood in austere silence.

Edward snapped on his cigarette lighter; he beamed it along the hòod to the door on the driver's side. Then followed by Murphy, slipped under the wheel and started the engine. There was the usual cough, a frantic shudder, and releasing the brakes Edward let the big car roll outside, where it waited panting for further instructions.

What now? Washington? The table around which the cabinet sat waiting for him to explain himself? Or perhaps *not* to explain himself! To hear himself saying: "I've no more to offer. I'm tired of trying to bring all of you around to my way of thinking: my simple Plan that frightens you because it *is* simple!" And the President smiling at that, twisting his fingers together and nodding solemnly. "I think you know, Edward, that I agree with you as far as my understanding goes. I think you are an unselfish servant of reality, a political physician carrying your panacea in a little black bag and distributing your Plan to a sick world, not really knowing whether it will work!" And then the rustle of amusement around the table . . . all the faces breaking into a sort of relieved embarrassment . . . "Well, thank God, we won't have to go along with him . . . no need to risk our necks just yet!" And the President, sensing a climax, saying: "I can't let you go, Edward!" And breaking off with a desperate look around the table hoping to find at least one sympathetic face. But failing. The others were shuffling their papers as if it were all decided . . . Edward was out of their hair, and they could return, each to his own convictions, safe and sound. The world wouldn't endure much longer anyway. It wasn't likely that they'd be around to witness the final crack-up, the

99

splitting asunder. So why assume something beyond their comprehension, only to be tripped by a national indifference? "Goodbye, Edward! We're glad to be rid of you but sorry to let you go . . ." The deteriorating earth rolls on its way . . . "An experiment like yours, Edward, might cast us all into chaos . . . Or it might so discipline and purify us as to make us over into solemn Puritans, existing according to the Plan, ignorant of sin and the ecstacy of repentance . . ."

The brief, unlikely vision passed. It wouldn't be like this at all! Once having stated his intention, his resignation would be politely received and promptly acted upon. After the preliminaries were done with, he'd leave Washington. He was still young enough to count on a third more of his life span. Where would he live? Not here at Easterly, certainly! What would he do with the years, provided, of course, there was no return to the death-compulsion? Would he write? Lecture? Teach? Travel?

He switched off the engine and sat in the dark, feeling momentarily safe as if the past were hermetically sealed within this elegant Pandora's box. Once he opened the car door the present would rush in again. And there he'd be . . . an ex-statesman faced with the job of becoming a man-like-any-other-man! His achievements would count for little with so many mistakes against him. He had failed. A single word: *carissima* . . . had destroyed confidence in his purpose: to give America a goal, a *reason* to sacrifice, to accomplish. He had failed, because he no longer believed in his own leadership. And suddenly he saw what it was he had wanted all along: *to be President*. And there was no hope of that now.

What was he doing, cowering in this decontamination chamber, this symbol of social superiority? This Rolls? Oh, God forgive him. Anger possessed him again! He switched on

100

the engine and into gear. The car began to climb toward Easterly, its tires crunching in the fallen crystals.

At the top of the hill he saw that the driveway was occupied by an immense silver bus, empty of passengers. Easterly's windows were tall squares of light. People inside were talking and laughing and someone seemed to be playing both pianos at once.

Edward parked the Rolls behind this behemoth of a bus and with Murphy at his heels ran up the steps to the open door. He hesitated there a moment, aware that he was shaking with the cold since he hadn't taken his overcoat. He must go inside and get it. Who in hell *were* all these people? Men. Twenty or thirty Whites, a few Negroes. Their overcoats were piled on a settee. They clustered near the hearth where someone had started a fire.

Then Edward saw Megan. He had somehow known that he would! She came along the corridor from the library and when she saw him broke into a little run. "Oh, I *hoped* you'd be here! I'm so glad . . ." And threw herself against him, her arms around his waist, and looked up at him with that flushed face of hers lifted as if she expected to be kissed. But Edward didn't oblige. Kissing, nowadays, was a TV ritual; everybody kissed at the drop of a hat. It had no meaning . . .

"I'm cold," he said.

She drew him away from the door into the hallway. All the man . . . they were dressed alike in traditional tuxedos... turned to stare at him.

"Here he is," Megan cried. "I told you we'd find him at home! Sir . . . Chris Dalton's orchestra. Never mind their names. They know yours, of course. Can I fix everybody a drink? I thought I shouldn't unless you were here . . ."

"Of course," Edward said.

Still with her arm around his waist, she steered him across to the cupboard where the best wines and liquors had been stored for three generations. Like fine books, dustless, handsome, they shone darkly on shelves all the way to the ceiling. Beneath, ranks of upside down glasses; beneath these, drawers for linen and silver. Not a bar in the usual sense . . . replacements made after each use preserved the look of a still-life, a picture painted by a Dutch master or tucked away in the background of a revel by Tiepolo.

Edward looked down at Megan. He expected to see the red sweater and the Cairn terrier hair, but this was the Megan Scott said could out-dress the Duchess of Windsor. She was wearing a black suit, very short. A frilled white waist with plaited cuffs that fell over her wrists. Her hair had been brushed back and up, twisted into a lofty Nefertiti coil, and this gave her childlike face an adult enchantment, as if the burnished black hair were meant to entice . . .

"Murphy, Murphy," she said, letting Edward go. And as she stooped to caress the excited dog, Edward noticed her fingers . . . polished, now, and painted. He reached for bottles and glasses. But he was still shaking, and made a mess of pouring. Megan took over. She dispensed the drinks to the men who crowded forward . . . there was no mistaking the aroma of the Scotch, the wood-like tang. The bourbon was softer, sweeter, and needed ice, had there been any . . . it had been customary to bring in bowls-full from the kitchen and then to smash the big chunks with a silver hammer. The last time . . . a year ago . . . and Edward wondered whether Valerie would have dispensed hospitality to these men? Probably not. Most of them were young, with abundant hair and voluptuous sideburns, rather stringy of body and pale-faced as men are who seldom see the sun. The Negroes were tall, with ink-black skin and pink palms, their fingernails very long and ivory white. They drank solemnly but without ceremony, displaying magnificent teeth when they smiled.

102

The Steinways trailed into silence and two young men came from the music room.

"Chris and Steve Dalton," Megan said, introducing them to Edward.

"Sir," they said in unison, offering him their pliant hands. They were perhaps in their thirties, very handsome and so much alike that Edward took them for twins. He thanked them for playing. "The pianos must have been grateful: no one ever touches them any more."

"Do you intend to leave them here, unplayed, all next winter?"

"They'll be swaddled like Eskimos," Edward interrupted, "during the winter . . . a man comes up from New York and sees to it. They hibernate."

"Good. We feel about great instruments as others feel about their children . . ."

Instantly aware that he had put his foot in it, the pianist moved away. The back of his neck was red; a slow flush attested to his chagrin. This was Edward's particular genius: to make the thoughtless aware of thoughtlessness, and to do it without a trace of rancor, a change of expression. He attached no blame to gaucheries he might have committed himself.

Megan put a glass in his hand . . . just the right amount; she wasn't the sort of woman to offer a brimming drink to get in the way of the teeth and to spill down the necktie or to bite rings in a fine table top.

"How did you get here?" Edward asked before he tasted. "And with these men? Who are they? You told me, but I've forgotten, if I ever knew. You see I'm not familiar with popular orchestras and their conductors . . . Set me straight."

"Enright found them for me," Megan said. "They are the *greatest*. They play all over the world to standing ovations . . . old fashionables and young hippies swooning in the aisles. Do you mean you've never heard of them?"

"I'm afraid not."

"They're on their way to Canada for some concerts before they fly overseas for a tour. At the last minute their publicity girl fell ill, and Enright recommended me. All done in half an hour! They *worship* you, by the way."

"Come now," Edward said.

"They do. So of course when I told them I'd like to stop off here and pick up Murphy, they agreed, because there was a chance of meeting *you*! So here we are! Here *I* am! They seem to like me, because during the long drive from New York I didn't utter a word . . . just sat and watched the windows and the lights flashing by and my own reflection in the glass. I thought I looked rather well, for me . . ."

"You do," Edward said. He asked whether the authorities would let her take Murphy overseas . . . did she know the English wouldn't admit dogs? They kept them in quarantine for six months.

"But we're going to the Continent, not to England. I can take Murphy! It's all understood and agreed to."

"I'm sorry," Edward said. "I've grown fond of him. Must you take him?"

Megan gave him a quick look. "I'm afraid I must. You see, he's mine."

"I suppose so."

"You can buy another dog, can't you?"

Edward turned away. Now he must surrender something else he loved and wanted! He was being stripped, like a plum that must be deprived of its skin before it is soft enough to chew and perhaps digest. He began to move among the guests, to say a few words to each in turn.

The drinks were easing any restraint they might have felt, and after a moment Edward knew that he, himself, was welcome.

The pianists returned to the Steinways and sent forth a shower of clean notes, one carrying a popular tune, the other setting the "beat." Noticing that a Negro was sitting alone on the stairs, Edward asked if he might sit there too. The Negro moved over and made room. He was fat . . . moist . . . with grizzled hair and fumed brown eyes. On his knees he held a brass instrument . . . Edward thought it was probably a trumpet . . . which he kept stroking. "Sit down. Sit down. Of course. Proud to have you."

"Thank you," Edward said.

Without seeming to, obliquely, the old man studied Edward's profile. Finally he said: "You're like him. Yes. If you'd grow a beard you'd be him to the life."

"I suppose you mean Lincoln? I've been told so often enough. I can't see it, myself. I've got his ugliness but not his wisdom."

He broke off and the Negro said: "I was watching you down there, how you spoke to the boys, and I thought maybe this is a part of him come back to have a look around. To see how things are."

"Things aren't so good," Edward said with a smile.

The Negro shook his head. He said: "Are you telling *me*? Things couldn't be worse. Remember when the astronauts stepped down on the moon? People said this was going to bring people together. But it hasn't happened."

Edward said: "What's that you've got there? A trumpet?"

"This? It's a horn. What used to be called a French horn. I learned it when I was a kid back in New Orleans fifty years ago. I've played it ever since. I was with Ellington for a long time. Now I'm with the Daltons." He put the instrument to his fat lips and blew a sustained note.

105

"How's *that*?"

"Wonderful," Edward said. "But it's a sweeter note than I've ever heard from a brass horn."

"That's no horn sound," the Negro said. "It's an Ellington sound. He taught me how to get it . . . not brass . . . velvet. . . You like it?"

"Very much. I've never liked a horn sound before. As a rule, it scratches my sensibilities. I guess I'm not musical-minded."

With a sudden, sharp look, the Negro said: "Neither was Lincoln. He liked country music. They say he sang off-key. But the songs he liked have lasted a hundred years. Not many today will last that long. 'Moon River' maybe, and 'Little Green Apples.' They speak to you. They say something. Kids on a silvery river. And a young fellow lucky in love . . ."

Edward looked down at the musicians, seeking Megan among them. Some of the men had apparently gone out to the bus for their instruments; there was a flash of metal, a sudden experimental tooting. A white-haired, scholarly looking fellow with spectacles set up a complex of bongos and began to tap and slap them.

The old Negro on the stairs said: "You ought to hear him when he plays the big drums. You know? When he cuts loose? He was with the Met . . . for years. He'd hop from one drum to another and put his ear down and get the pitch and then whack the daylight out of the things. Remember *Parsifal?*"

"I'm afraid not."

"You ought to hear more music."

"I've never had time," Edward admitted with a twinge of shame as if he had revealed a character defect in himself. "When I was a boy my parents made me sit through symphony concerts, but it didn't take. I heard more music

106

before I was ten than I could hold. I learned not to listen. I slept away years in the family box at Carnegie Hall."

"Poor little fellow," the old Negro said. "What *did* you enjoy?"

"Reading."

"There you have me. I can't read or write."

"I don't believe you."

"It's true."

"You sound like an educated man."

"I am. But I never went to school."

"Your accent. You're from the Barbados, aren't you? You sound like an Englishman."

"I'm not. I was born here in America, in Lousisiana. We were a big family. Twelve brothers and sisters, four grandparents and our mother and father, all living in one room . . . if you could call it a room. When I was ten, I ran away to New Orleans. Believe it or not I was a good-looking boy . . . like a ripe cherry! Girls were always after me. But when I was fifteen, I fell in love with this . . ."

He stroked the bright object on his knees.

"Somebody had thrown it into a trash dump! I'll never forget the first time it spoke to me . . . all rusty as it was . . . yet in a voice so sweet . . . *So sweet!* It sounded all through me from head to toes! I began to hang around the little dark places, polishing the musician's shoes for them, running errands, anything to be near them. To hear them building the music of the future."

"No school, eh?" Edward said.

"School? For a ragged little black like me? I used to watch the Catholic children, herded by nuns, very prim and snobbish about God. And the public schools sucking in their pupils at eight in the morning, spewing them out in the afternoon . . . they'd tumble down the steps, carrying their books, and if the boys happened to see me they fell on me

107

and beat me up."

There was a pause. Then Edward said quietly: "Because you were black."

"I learned that lesson early."

Edward was silent. He thought back to his "tutored" days . . . the years at Groton . . . Harvard . . . the Sorbonne . . .

"I still don't understand," he said finally. "Are you trying to tell me you're self-taught?"

The old Negro chuckled. It was a "fat" sound; it had the consistency of custard. He picked up the horn and blew softly into the mouthpiece, feeling his way into the chaos below. Joining it. The music began to take form. Edward knew enough to realize that it wasn't like any music he'd ever heard. There seemed to be two levels of sound: melody on top, accompaniment below. The men played while walking around the room, breaking off long enough to sip their drinks, then setting the glasses down again, to join the others. Easterly gathered itself around this wild cacophony and Murphy, frightened, ran up to put his head on Edward's knee.

Megan was dancing with a fellow whose bearded chin made him look like a smiling goat. He had huge hands, immense feet and danced with grace and ease. Megan came scarcely to his waist. Both of them kept their eyes closed and crocheted their way around the room, never dropping a stitch. And Edward thought that Easterly must be stirring out of its sleep, cracking its old bones, stretching its atrophied muscles. The house had survived too long, and might soon disintegrate from lack of use . . . those who could prevent its dissolution were abdicating, joining the mob, looking about for stones to hurl at "Order"; to bring down the weakened walls of American elegance.

Suddenly Megan opened her eyes and as she passed close to the steps where Edward sat gave him a look that seemed to

108

penetrate his cold heart. It had happened like this once before . . . a quick look and she shut her eyes again. But it was the woman look and, there could be no doubt, it was meant for him. *Carissima* . . . Oh, God . . .

The Negro said: "You took me for an educated man. I am. But not schooled."

"How was it done?"

"I have good hearing," the Negro said. He paused and with an almost maternal gesture, as if he coddled a child, lifted the horn and held it against his breast. "I was lucky. I wanted to learn. And I found a way."

"Ah," Edward said.

"Not what you think. Not school."

"What then?"

"I was fifteen when I found a teacher. I'm seventy-five now. We lived together almost fifty years. She was a white woman. Very beautiful . . ." The Negro broke off. "Have you ever been on the 'street of women' in New Orleans?"

"Yes. An alley. Dark and filthy. Shacks on both sides. The doors open and girls standing on the thresholds beneath red lamps. I remember very well. I was fifteen myself. I went there with some of my classmates on a lark. We were all scared to death." Edward looked sharply into the old man's face. *"Why?"* he asked. "Why there?"

"I'll tell you something I've never told anyone . . . I was cornered outside this white woman's house one night . . . stabbed and bruised and covered with sticky blood. She took me in and cared for me for a long time. I lay on her bed, half conscious, while she slept on the floor. She had no business all that time. Men pounded on her door but she kept it locked and turned off the red light that advertised what she was. There's a name for such women, but I've never used it

109

and I never shall. She had been married to a man she loved and had been deceived by him. She left him and her family up North and no one ever heard of her again. They finally took it she had killed herself. And in a way she had. She earned enough to keep life in her body, but that was all and it was enough for her. She had no wish to be what she was born to be: a lady. Being a lady had been a great disappointment."

"She was older than you?"

"Ten years older."

"I suppose by now she's gone . . . you say you're seventy . . ."

"Close as I can guess. I was a bright boy and she knew life was going to be hard on me. I wanted to know things and was always asking her questions . . . about the earth and the stars and Man . . . So she set out to teach me. She had had what's known as 'every advantage.' French and German governesses when she was a child. Then private school in Washington . . . a school run for little swells . . . daughters of men important in public life. She had a proper debut. Long white gloves and flowers in her hair . . ."

The old man broke off. He reached into his pocket for a handkerchief, unfolded the spotless square and mopped his drenched, black-ivory face.

"Her hair. You never saw such hair: silver gold and down to her waist."

"Well," Edward said. "What happened then?"

"She taught me everything she knew and then went on to study what other people knew. She got hold of books and read aloud to me . . . years and years I listened and most of the time I understood. She was a great teacher. She could put history together so that I knew what came when . . . art and music, science and religion. She taught me how to *think* historically, not in little bits and pieces but in great *wedges*,

110

great slices . . . do you know what I mean?"

Edward nodded. But he said nothing.

"When I got started in music, she helped me there, too. So I began to play *this* . . ." He touched the horn. "I played intelligently. In my head, I could hear all the music of the ages. I didn't need the mathematics of it . . . I had the dream. And I climbed straight up to the top. I guess in my way I'm as famous as you are."

"You don't take fame seriously, I hope?"

"Yes. I do. It means something. It means you're unique. And do you know what it did for me? I didn't resent being black! She saw to that. I never thought of myself as anything or anybody but *me*! So I was spared hating. I kept away from people as much as I could. When they saw I didn't need them, didn't care *what* they thought of me, they wanted me. I could have played in any orchestra in the world. But Ellington had what I liked and now the Daltons. She taught me how to live inside myself. You're like that, aren't you?"

"I must be. I'm mortally afraid of criticism." Edward, with a shake of his head, cast off the realization. "I cannot understand," he said, "why this remarkable woman failed to teach you how to read and write."

"She wanted me to need her. I was her only friend; she was growing old when, at last, she died."

"How did she die?"

"I came back from a show one night to find the red light smashed and policemen and an ambulance and she herself, white as chalk, lying flat on her bed, her hands folded, her face peaceful. And the room cluttered with *books, books, books!*"

Edward looked down at Megan as she came close to the foot of the stairs again. He thought of the pale woman on her shameful bed who had given most of her life to a man she

111

was forbidden to love. A man she had taught not to be implicated in the terrible problems of his race, as she had retreated from her own . . . And Megan? Was she the other side of the medal? Did she waken every morning expecting rapture? What made her so rosy and bright-eyed and laughing? Was she capable of pity? Concern for the men she enslaved? Why had she come for Murphy? Why? To be rid of a debt? To write off the hundred dollars Edward had given her . . . perhaps to wipe off Murphy himself in a few days? What was the word: *collateral*? Perhaps she had used the big dog over and over again when she needed money? Perhaps Scott had been wrong in his opinion of her, captured by her gaiety as men are when netted by familiarity.

Murphy whined; torn between the man he had learned to love and the woman who had neglected him but had never bored him, he tore down to leap against her, grinning from ear to ear . . .

This time, Megan failed to look up at Edward. Another man tapped her partner and claimed her. They began not to dance but to gyrate like twigs on a tree torn by a gusty wind. Standing apart, without grace or rhythm, they twisted their torsos, jerked their heads, lifted and shook their arms; they looked like half-wit damn fools. Victims of St. Vitus' dance, Edward decided. He had always loathed this exhibitionism and had hoped that by now it would have lost its popularity. Once he himself had tried it and had come off from the battle with a strained sacroiliac and a stiff neck. It was not for him. And, watching Megan involved in these convulsions, he suffered a return of disgust and anger. He turned back to the old Negro.

"Thank you for telling me about your teacher," he said. "But I'm afraid I don't believe a word of it. You expected me to be both attentive and credulous? You forget that my life has been dedicated to tracking down the truth. I confess I've

112

come up with little of the authentic stuff . . . Just as we were disappointed when the moon turned out to be made not of cheese but of gray talcum powder, we're beginning to doubt the rest of our beliefs. So I find it hard to be credulous. Forgive me."

The Negro laughed his custardy laugh. "You don't fool *me*," he said, mopping his face again. "You *want* to believe me. But something's wrong with you! You don't accept the truth of love."

Edward considered this. After a moment he said, "I'm not conditioned to fantasy."

He looked away from Megan writhing in that obscene ritual in the hall below and put both hands over his eyes.

"Your story leaves me cold. If it were true, it would be a marvelous thing, and should be known to mankind . . . You told it to me and I can't believe it, as perhaps you hoped I would?"

"You needn't," the old Negro said. He lifted the shining horn and began to play. As if at a signal, the pianists slipped into a waltz and after a few bars a song began, a romantic song, very slow, with pauses when the waltz predominated for a moment. Then the song took over. The other musicians no longer accompanied the pianos. Megan and her partner moved away from the stairs and crossed to the cupboard . . . all the glasses were refilled and drained . . . The clock on the mantel struck eleven. And someone said: "Time to be getting along. There's a blizzard. We'll never make it unless we go now."

Edward let his hands slide down across his face. The premonition had taken hold of his mind again. He felt the beginning of the compulsion, the pressure inside his skull. In an effort to save himself from disaster, he said: "What *is* that you're playing?"

The Negro dropped the horn again.

"I'm glad you asked. It means it got to you."

"It did."

"The waltz is by Chopin. The song is by Giordano. From his opera *Fedora* . . . You speak Italian?"

"Yes."

"It begins: *La tua man' lieva, fra le mie man'!* Your fragile hands between mine . . . Chris Dalton wrote the arrangement."

"Keep on," Edward said, "to the end."

"Another time. When you're in the White House, invite me to play for you there. If Casals could, I can!"

The Negro gave Edward's hand a moist clasp.

"I'll hear from you," he said.

Edward was on the point of confessing that the White House was no longer in his own plans for the future. He shook his head but let the remark pass. Seeing that the musicians were getting their overcoats, he went down and across the room to Megan.

She made him wait a moment while she poured a drink for him. He refused it with a "Thank you, but no . . . I'm leaving in a few moments. I'll be driving."

"I hope we haven't upset you, barging in like this? So late?"

"No."

The others were streaming through the door and out to the bus. A few of them threw a "good night" in his direction, but no one stopped to thank him for his hospitality. The twin pianists shrugged themselves into heavy coats with high Edwardian collars; they followed the others, carrying themselves with a cocksure slant of their heads, hands busy with gaudy silk scarves which they twisted around their necks and tucked in. As they stepped outside, their shoulders were instantly powdered with snow . . . They disappeared toward the bus which flashed on its headlights.

114

"They're great, aren't they?" Megan said. She wouldn't meet Edward's eyes and he had a feeling that she was disappointed in him. Perhaps she had wanted him to dance with her . . . take her off into a corner and whisper to her . . . instead, he had spent half an hour sitting beside an unprepossessing black man, halfway up the stairs, well out of her reach!

"I'm afraid we've made a mess of it," she said, glancing around at the uncorked bottles and empty glasses. "I'm sorry."

"It will all be taken care of in the morning . . ." Edward began. He broke off, aware that this simple statement sounded pretentious, and said rather lamely: "I was very glad to see you."

"Now you're laughing at me!"

"No."

She reached down to Murphy and hooked her fingers under the big dog's collar.

"Thanks for taking such good care of him," she said.

"I wish you'd leave him here with me," Edward began, unable to control a note of pleading in his voice.

"I couldn't. Not possibly."

Outside, the bus sounded a warning and Megan turned to follow the last stragglers. Murphy objected. He strained against her hand so that the collar slipped down over his eyes.

"You see," Edward said, "he doesn't *want* to go."

"He'll get over it," she said.

Suddenly Edward's suffering, that had been building toward a climax, took over his consciousness. He was filled with resentment, so profound a reaction that he lost all control over his behavior. He shouted at Megan: "Have you forgotten our agreement? You used the word *collateral* . . . how easily you sidestep your given word! Like most women you have no honor . . . you're a cheat, damn you!"

115

Megan hesitated then dragged Murphy away and without a backward look, went out into the blue-white dark. The bus headlights swung then pointed down the drive. Edward stood looking after the blurring taillights, as he had once before this day. He could still hear his own voice shouting: "You're a cheat! Damn you!"

And so she was. She had taken Murphy and had broken her word. With a vicious kick Edward closed the door and went to stand before the fire. He had never in his life cursed a woman . . . Why had he lost his temper like this? His self-control? Was it the dog, really? Or Megan's indifference? Or was it that hundred dollars? Good God! He hoped not!

The untouched drink was within reach; he drank all of it, the glass rattling against his teeth. The liquid burned on the way down, then spread into his veins. He went to the door, opened it and hurled the glass into the dark. He heard it shatter in the drive.

The Rolls waited. Eyebrows of snow hung over the roof, thatched it. There wasn't a breath of wind. And Edward decided that he'd make it safely through, at least as far as the freeway, if he started at once. He turned back and ran upstairs to his bedroom for the suitcase. Then down again and along the corridor to the library. He must turn off the lamp!

As he reached for the switch he noticed Scott's portrait of Megan and on an impulse lifted it for a closer look. Tucked under the heavy beaver-board he found a hundred dollar bill.

Ignoring the downstairs lights, he ran outside and across to the Rolls. The bus tracks were still visible. He thought he knew which road it would take. If it refused to stop for him, he'd maneuver the Rolls into its path. All he wanted was to clean the slate with Megan. Now his hatred was directed against himself. Yet his outburst had, in a way, steadied him.

116

Taking command of the wheel with hands that seemed frozen with determination, he pushed the Rolls through the open gate. Peering through the windshield, where the wipers had cleaned U-shaped wedges of clear glass, he saw Megan. She was climbing toward him, Murphy beside her.

Edward drew off the road, braked, and ran down to her, slipping and sliding in the snow. Her face was streaming wet and she was very pale; the coil of hair had come loose; the black suit, soaked through, clung to her body. She had no top-coat, no gloves. She was carrying a small square satchel. Edward took it out of her hand. "Let me," he said.

"Thank you . . . They couldn't wait for me, so I promised I'd catch up with them by plane tomorrow. It was stupid of me to leave the money hidden like that . . ."

"Get in the car," Edward said. "You'll stay the night. Come, Murphy. *In!*"

Murphy obeyed. His puzzled eyes sought the truth of these humans: to which one did he belong? Why these awful moments of indecision? Which one wanted him? Which one loved him? What next?

Edward swung the car back on the road, drove to a safe turn-around and headed toward Easterly. The snow was falling very softly yet heavily . . . already the fences along the road were disappearing.

Megan seemed very small beside Edward, but perhaps she was crouching a little, holding her arms around herself but getting no warmth that way. She chattered.

"We'll be home in a minute," Edward said. Only after he'd said it did he wonder how "home" got into what was meant to be a friendly speech. Megan looked up at him, quick and puzzled.

"Cheers," she said. He was beginning to realize that "cheers" was one of her favorite words, used to punctuate every situation. It was a sort of verbal exclamation point.

117

Cheers! Well . . . better than *carissima* . . .

The hallway had already rid itself of music; the last of the cigarette smoke eddied along the ceiling; the fire was blazing its last. Megan went close to the warmth and watched while Edward added another log and some cones that exploded and crackled. There was a sudden smell of hot pine; it made Edward think of his lean-to in the forest, his bed of aromatic boughs, fresh-stripped. And of boyhood . . .

Megan could shift from sleek elegance to a state of dishevelment beyond description. She did this now.

"I'll get you a blanket," Edward said.

He ran upstairs to the bedroom, a little surprised that Murphy hadn't followed him. Poor Murphy. He didn't, at the moment, belong to anyone.

Edward jerked the red satin quilt off the bed and holding it at arms' length hurried downstairs.

"Let me wrap this around you," he said. "When you've had something to eat you can go upstairs and get out of these wet clothes. You'll find a closet full of my country things. They smell of camphor but they're dry."

"Thank you," Megan said. She held out her hand and he took it. *"La tua man' lieva fra le mie man'."* He thought he could hear Giordano's song again, but that of course was his imagination.

"Will you forgive me?" he said.

"For what?"

"For seeming to doubt your word. I didn't give a damn about the money . . ."

She shook her head. "You called me a cheat because you thought I was. But I'm not! I didn't promise that you could keep Murphy forever. You said I could have him back whenever I asked for him. I didn't know how much you needed him. He's yours. He rates belonging to a great man.

118

He's a great dog."

"He is," Edward said. "We'll share him, shall we? I mean a sort of part time arrangement? He can stay with me when I'm at home and with you when *you* are. Fair enough? It's just that being alone is a problem."

"You needn't be alone," Megan said.

He let go of her hand and went back to the fireplace. After a moment he remarked that he was of small use to anyone at the moment. "My mind has a habit of slipping into confusion. Murphy doesn't know this. He doesn't care. It's enough for him, just having me around."

"He's a sharp dog," Megan remarked. "It would be enough for me, too . . . just having you around."

"It could be arranged," Edward said. To cover his confusion he went to the kitchen, found the cold chicken Mrs. Littlefield had mentioned and a bowl of potato salad.

It seemed that Megan wasn't hungry, after all. Neither was Edward. Picking at the food, he blamed this on a lifelong aversion to eating poultry. When he was a youngster, the farmers in the neighborhood of Easterly let their chickens wander wherever there were insects or pebbles or foolish, languorous butterflies pulsing on the grass. Edward remembered the sudden flurries of panic, the hens taking off for no apparent reason, the chicks blown in pursuit like dried leaves in the wind. And then the long, hot summer afternoons when the little flocks bedded down in the shade to sleep. Edward always suffered a faint nausea when he cut off a slice of chicken breast. He ate, but without appetite, as if he were chewing on the repository of a brave heart. Yet chickens were said to be cannibalistic . . . if he could only convince himself of that . . .!

He put the plate aside.

"I'm not hungry," he said.

119

"It's my fault," Megan protested. "I've upset you."

"Yes. You have."

"How? Tell me, sir. What have I done?"

"You baited your hook with a trick. That money hidden where I might not find it for days, if ever! Was that fair? Suddenly you tore me off that bloody hook and tossed me back. I had to discover for myself that you're as honest as my sainted grandmother!"

"I am," Megan said. And as an afterthought: "My! What a temper!"

After a pause Edward said: "I don't know what to make of you. How to deal with you . . ."

"You said it yourself, sir. I'm as honest as your sainted grandmother . . ."

"I guess tonight was the wrong time to put *me* to the test, then," Edward said. "I was on the verge of an explosion and you lighted the fuse. I blew, that's all. Nothing on earth could have stopped me."

Megan smiled.

"We're quite a pair, aren't we? Could it be that we're . . . attracted?"

"Here," he said, "give me that plate! You'll find my room at the top of the stairs. I'll be up in a minute . . ."

But almost at once he followed her.

She said, "You know, I *am* cold. There's a big storm outside. I can feel it. Heavy and soft and already deep. We couldn't leave now even if we wanted to."

"We don't want to," Edward said. "Don't worry. I'll get you started in the morning in time to catch up with your musicians. They're probably stalled somewhere . . . a bus stop, we hope, where they can find coffee and shelter. There's one about thirty miles down the road."

"Cheers," she said.

120

Vaguely relieved by the need to turn his back on her, he searched in a closet for something she might wear. But even his jackets would have engulfed her. And the overcoats looked like Prussian Field-Marshals. There was, however, a terry cloth bathrobe that must have belonged to one of his sons. The touch of it made Edward wince. But he handed it to Megan.

"Put this on," he said. "Then come downstairs. I'll have a hot drink ready for you."

"Thank you, sir."

"Sir?"

"What *should* I call you?"

He stared at her a moment then turned away and left the room, slamming the door.

Down in the hallway Murphy lay on the hearth. Exhausted by divided loyalties, all he would allow Edward was a thwack of his tail.

The robe was too large for Megan; she had wrapped it around herself and had lashed it firmly at the waist with the cord. She was a Cairn terrier again, her eyes shining through a fringe of bang.

"What happened to Nefertiti?" Edward asked.

"Nefertiti? Oh, you mean the wig! I left it on the bed post." She curled herself up in one of the sofas flanking the fire. Her feet were bare but she made no effort to cover them. "I know," she said, "I'll call you Edward. Would you like that!"

"I'd like it very much," Edward said.

"Thank you, Edward . . . Oh, no. I *can't*! Not *Edward*! It's not what I feel about you." She patted the sofa. "Sit down. Or don't you ever?"

"Sometimes," Edward said. "But I like to prowl." He stood above her, looking, looking at her, suddenly unable to

121

come closer.

"I know," she said finally. "I'll just keep on calling you 'sir'."

"It seems rather formal."

"Sir Lancelot," she said. "Sir Galahad . . . No. It's not formal. It's romantic."

"Come now!"

"Please sit down."

He hand't fixed a drink for himself, and this now offered an excuse to leave the room.

When he came back, the glass burning his fingers, he found that Megan hadn't finished her own drink, but sat holding it between cupped hands. How small she was! How lovely in her way . . . the luminous whiteness of her throat in contrast to her flushed face . . . her lips and cheeks stained with the "veritable raspberry" of youth and good health.

"Your drink's cold now," he said.

"Not quite," she said, and drank it to the last drop.

"Another?"

"Thank you," she said. "No. You see, I'm always intoxicated! It's cheaper than Scotch. You drain your imagination, but there's always more where it came from."

She leaned back in the sofa again, looking around the room as if seeing it for the first time.

"Were you born here?" she asked. And when Edward nodded, she went on: "It's not beautiful, really. But proud and splendid. Was it presumptuous of me to bring those men here uninvited?"

"I thought them very adaptable," Edward said. "They might have been bored, but they seemed to enjoy themselves."

"They did. What were you and Slippery Elm talking about?"

"Is *that* his name?"

122

Edward felt an inward spasm of laughter. He explained that the Negro had confided in him; he was sorry but he didn't feel free to repeat anything that was said. He didn't solicit confessions; they happened to him. He had learned to snap the lock on what he was told and he was fairly sure he could be trusted to throw the key away. This, to their amazed delight, strangers discovered when they were alone with him. No longer thrown by his reputation they revealed their most secret selves, later to boast: "He's not hard to know at all. I believe I can claim to be his friend. We talked for hours, although to tell the truth I can't remember that he said anything. *I* did all the talking!"

Megan gave him her empty glass and he put it beside his own on the coffee table. He felt the warm liquor in his veins; a speed-up of circulation, a pounding of the blood in his temples. What did she expect of him? What did she want of him? And he was abruptly aware of being alone with her. And of that look in her eyes, the woman look he had abjured for so long . . . it was meant for him . . .

There must have been a gust of wind because suddenly the fire puffed out a belch of smoke and the snow crystals struck hard against the window panes. Easterly creaked from room to room, then settled again and Edward and Megan heard the rush of the blizzard.

"Where did it come from?" Megan asked. "A minute ago there wasn't a breath of wind . . ."

"Easterly's withstood almost a century of storms like this," Edward said. "Once we had a gale that flattened acres of forest . . . sheared the trees so that they cracked and fell, all in the same direction."

"I'm not afraid," Megan said.

Edward crossed to one of the windows and rubbed a pane with his coat sleeve. Something Megan had said triggered the

123

memory of that Charleston hurricane and Valerie telling the boys that their father would get them safely home, to trust him. Trying to conceal his utter dismay he went from window to window drawing the heavy curtains, muffling the mournful howl of the storm.

"We're safe here," he said at last and turned back into the room.

"I know," Megan said. "You'll see to that."

For a moment they listened to the slam of the wind against the house, the thud of snow falling from the roof into the canvas awnings over the porch. Then Edward shifted the heavy fire screen and kicked at the logs, rolling them back so that the smoke found a way up the chimney again. Kneeling there, he fought the familiar battle with the headache that always gave advance notice of his will to die.

He heard Megan say: "Being here is like being inside a time capsule! This isn't *now*. It's *then*. Right smack in the center of the Victorian fifty-years-of-peace! It's hard to believe, isn't it, that out there America's at war with itself? This quiet, strong house and the snow . . ."

She broke off.

"I wish," she said after a moment, "it would last forever. Won't you arrange it, sir?"

"I?"

"You could. There's nothing you can't do."

He got to his feet.

"How about saving the country?" he said, forcing himself to smile. "Cleaning up the whole mess single-handed?"

"You could. You will. Weren't you on your way to Washington when I came back?"

"Yes."

"You have some sort of Plan," Megan began.

"Who hasn't?"

"Everyone's talking about it, but no one seems to know

124

what it is. Can you tell me?"

"No," Edward said.

And then, to temper his refusal, he said: "I could invent one, if it would amuse you. How about razing the great cities and building walled towns all over the United States? A sort of conglomerate of principalities, each one self-contained . . ."

"Oh, stop it," Megan cried. "I'm *not* amused." She patted the sofa. "I'm developing a whiplash from looking up at that wonderful face of yours. *Please* sit down."

He surrendered and sat beside her. The pain behind his eyes was building to the moment of utter loss of control. Megan seemed to sense that he was suffering; she reached out and with the tips of her fingers stroked his forehead.

"That wonderful face of yours," she repeated.

Edward closed his eyes and felt her pressing lightly on his lids . . . and then down to his lips, his chin, his throat and around to the back of his neck and into his hair. He could have kissed her but the opportunity lasted a second too long; all he could manage was his arm across her shoulders, heavy and tight. They sat like this, in silence, their breathing shallow and fast as if they had run a long race. As indeed they had.

Murphy started from sleep, attacked a flea on his muzzle, turned twice around then stretched out again. He could wait. He must wait a little longer now.

5

When the telephone in the library rang, Edward was tempted to let it go unanswered. But the sound was imperative; he reacted to it as he always had and, withdrawing his arm from around Megan he hurried along the corridor toward that familiar bell, that dry, precise voice:

"Edward? Ah! You're there! I was anxious because I was under the impression that you left Easterly at six o'clock . . . Are you all right?"

"Yes. But I can't get out. This is quite a storm . . . ."

"Are you alone?"

Edward hesitated. He avoided a direct answer, and said that if it were necessary he could always call on the caretakers who lived in the village, but would come if he needed them . . .

He went on quickly to ask why in heaven's name had he been under such close surveillance?

"Surveillance? No such orders were given here! The county

127

patrol was instructed to keep an eye on you. But no one else
. . ."

"Not the F.B.I.?"

"Of course not!"

Edward said that he could understand the influx of
cameramen on his first morning at Easterly. They were no
trouble and perhaps the publicity did more good than harm.
But when·he was away at Scott's studio, the place swarmed
with a sort of search party, ten or fifteen men beating the
bushes and peering into every cupboard and closet in the
house.

"I can't understand it," the familiar voice interrupted.
"You were to be left alone. On your own. I hoped under the
circumstances you'd realize your strength and stop grieving
over the irrevocable . . ."

At that instant, with a sharp click, the phone went dead
and every light in the house blacked out.

Edward stood for a moment in sudden, engulfing dark; he
fumbled for some response from Washington:

"Hello? Hello?"

Nothing. Nothing except the snow against the windows,
which from this angle of the house sounded like a frantic
rattle of bead portieres. There was a flicker of reflected
firelight along the corridor and Edward hurried back to the
hallway.

Megan was sitting up. Her eyes flashed at him as he came
toward her. The room was very dark and suddenly very cold.

"What was that?"

"Washington," he said briefly. "But they were cut off. The
wires must be down . . ."

She seemed to relax then. But when he put his hand on her
shoulder he could feel her shivering.

"I'm going to take you upstairs," he said, "and put you to
bed."

128

She didn't resist and, leaning over her, he gathered her into his arms and lifted her. She was very light, almost weightless, as if he carried an imagined woman. But she said nothing, neither protested nor laughed, only relaxed against him and gave herself to the quick climb, her head against his shoulder. There was no excitement in this contact, only a sort of surprise, as if he were dreaming a reality. If anything, he was afraid. Afraid because this might have been Valerie, as he remembered carrying her away from the wrecked plane. But Valerie was dead. This woman was alive, alive and in his arms. And there was no hideous guilt to confuse him and send him half falling, staggering to his feet again, stumbling in circles until the rescuers took Valerie away from him . . . This time he climbed quickly and easily up the long flight of carpeted stairs, pushing the Valerie image out with a powerful thrust of his will to forget for once and for all, to have done with it forever . . .

Murphy had followed and when Edward put Megan down on the bed, the big dog crossed politely to the hearth and lay there, watching but not interfering, as if he sensed that something must be decided between this man and woman . . . He, too, was shivering . . . little ripples ran beneath his smooth black coat; it was partly the chill of the room and partly his dog-nerves, so alert to human behavior . . . Covering Megan with the red quilt, Edward found matches and built a fire using the odd sticks Mr. Littlefield had left for him. He tried to believe that Megan was asleep . . . if she were, he could go quietly away and wait for dawn and, he supposed, be grateful for the chance to conquer the tide of feeling rising within him, taking over, licking at his senses like the flames that sprang from the match he held to the dry kindling. He knelt there, and did not once look toward the bed.

Then, at last, Megan made the decision. She said:
"Lie with me."
That was all. "Lie with me." In such a gentle voice, almost
a whisper, almost as if he hadn't really heard. He got to his
feet and went to her, pulling the quilt back and then
unfastening the cord that closed the small, terrycloth robe
and peeling the robe back as you might strip a flower's petals,
revealing her whiteness . . .
She reached up to him, her arms around his neck, and
pulled him down to dare at last to kiss her.
"Lie with me," she whispered again. "I want you. I love
you."

For a long time the storm of their feeling and the storm
outside engulfed them . . . there was only the surge of love
and the rage of wind and snow . . . they were burning, but
not consumed . . . Together, they suffered exultation and
then sank into brief respites, when they renewed their need
and their purpose; to climb again, to struggle again, to
achieve again. And never to be sated or disappointed. Megan
was a lover who yielded, but still withheld an exciting
promise of more to give. She made Edward aware of his own
incomparable body, for so many years unrecognized and
rebuffed. The women he had known intimately had always
cheated him of victory. Was it because they feared to match
their lack against his abundance, to be found out if they
surrendered themselves to a superior male? Or did his
reticence chill them? Their response was flattering, but never
complete. Megan let him know the width and depth and
height of her feeling. When in moments of calm, they lay
together, she still held him close and closer, whispering that
she had loved him for as long as she could remember and
would love him beyond the rim of the earth, to be aware of
him in space . . . in time . . . in mind and in soul . . . But she

130

didn't ask him if he loved her, and he didn't say; he made love, and there was no need to say. She wasn't a woman to ask for proof or to demand reassurance when neither was lacking.

He thought: *I will marry her. There will be more of this . . . and more.* And he knew why he had fought so long for eminence . . . not to dazzle Megan, but to share with her, to go on climbing with her beside him. She would encourage him, and believe in him as Valerie had never believed in him . . . At the thought of Valerie, the word *carissima* flashed across his mind . . . He flung himself on his side out of Megan's arms, and would have wept if he had been capable of weeping.

"What is it?" Megan said. "Tell me. What have I done?"

He turned back to her. "Nothing. I was thinking how much I've missed. How many years without you. There's so little time left . . . Don't leave me again."

Megan was silent for a moment. Then she said: "I might. I'm restless. I wouldn't marry you if you asked me, sir! Because I'd spoil things for you. I don't belong in your world. I couldn't keep step with you. But if you ever need me, I'll come. From wherever I am. Whatever I'm doing. A letter. A wire. A phone call from you and I'll be on my way. Go to Washington and make that Plan of yours work . . . I'll be watching every step you take. And remembering tonight. I love you."

"We'll see," Edward said. "I can be very persuasive. And persistent. But I'll let you go free if that's what you want."

"That's what I want." She reached up with her small fingers and touched his lips. "Let me sleep now . . ."

It was eleven o'clock when Edward woke to a room full of white, blinding sunlight. Megan was not there. The red coverlet lay on the floor beside the bed and she had tossed her pillow down, too; it still bore the imprint of her head.

131

Edward went to the window. The storm had passed, leaving the world buried under immaculate snow. Not a rabbit or a fox track . . . not a bird print, as far as the eye could reach. Somewhere on the other side of the house there was a noisy chugging . . . snow ploughs moving up the drive, perhaps. Somehow he knew that Megan wasn't out there . . . she had "hitched" a ride into the village and away . . . But he heard Murphy's excited barking . . .

He stood at the window for a long time, aware of being alive and being happy. Happiness had always eluded him; he had never experienced it until now. He was loved. What a simple answer to the great enigma! He was loved! He stretched to his full height, naked in the snow-light, proud of himself, and loved. The world out there was more beautiful than he had ever imagined it could be. He felt delight in the contour of the land, the blackness of the pines, the lake, the clean sky . . . He was Man, fulfilled. He pounded his chest with both clenched fists. And going into the bathroom, examined his reflection in the mirror. This time he didn't hate his face. He lathered, and shaved, and dressed. Then he hurried down to the library, slipped Scott's portrait of Megan in his suitcase, and went out to the driveway where Murphy leaped to lick his hands. The ploughs were tossing lofty arcs of snow and Mr. Littlefield was freeing the patient Rolls of its thick white robe.

"All ready," he said when he saw Edward, "you can get started any minute now . . . The roads are free below . . ."

www.ingramcontent.com/pod-product-compliance
Lightning Source LLC
Chambersburg PA
CBHW011507170626
46812CB00008B/3003